In accepting a bed for the night and now a job, Leonie had been given a tiny taste of what her life could be like off the streets.

Of having a shower whenever she wanted it, of having clean sheets and clean clothes. Of having food brought to her and something to do that wasn't figuring out how to shoplift her next meal, or begging for coins. Of being safe behind walls and locked doors.

Just a tiny taste. Enough to know she didn't want to give it up, not just yet.

This is how they suck you in. You should have run...

She swallowed, clutching her cleaning implements even tighter. It was too late to run now, too late to decide that the streets were better than being in this house and working for this duke. Like Persephone from myth, she'd had a bite of the pomegranate, and now she was trapped in the underworld.

Which makes Cristiano Hades.

Yes, and a very fine Hades he made, too. No wonder she found him dangerous. He was the snake in the garden, offering temptation...

Jackie Ashenden writes dark, emotional stories with alpha heroes who've just gotten the world to their liking only to have it blown apart by their kick-ass heroines. She lives in Auckland, New Zealand, with her husband, the inimitable Dr. Jax, two kids and two rats. When she's not torturing alpha males and their gutsy heroines, she can be found drinking chocolate martinis, reading anything she can lay her hands on, wasting time on social media or being forced to go mountain biking with her husband. To keep up-to-date with Jackie's new releases and other news, sign up to her newsletter at jackieashenden.com.

Books by Jackie Ashenden

Harlequin Presents

Crowned at the Desert King's Command

Shocking Italian Heirs

Demanding His Hidden Heir
Claiming His One-Night Child

Visit the Author Profile page
at Harlequin.com for more titles.

Jackie Ashenden

THE SPANIARD'S WEDDING REVENGE

HARLEQUIN

PRESENTS

If you purchased this book without a cover you should be aware that this book is stolen property. It was reported as "unsold and destroyed" to the publisher, and neither the author nor the publisher has received any payment for this "stripped book."

HARLEQUIN®
PRESENTS®

Recycling programs
for this product may
not exist in your area.

ISBN-13: 978-1-335-14856-8

The Spaniard's Wedding Revenge

Copyright © 2020 by Jackie Ashenden

All rights reserved. No part of this book may be used or reproduced in any manner whatsoever without written permission except in the case of brief quotations embodied in critical articles and reviews.

This is a work of fiction. Names, characters, places and incidents are either the product of the author's imagination or are used fictitiously. Any resemblance to actual persons, living or dead, businesses, companies, events or locales is entirely coincidental.

This edition published by arrangement with Harlequin Books S.A.

For questions and comments about the quality of this book, please contact us at CustomerService@Harlequin.com.

Harlequin Enterprises ULC
22 Adelaide St. West, 40th Floor
Toronto, Ontario M5H 4E3, Canada
www.Harlequin.com

Printed in U.S.A.

THE SPANIARD'S
WEDDING REVENGE

To Justin Alastair, Duke of Avon, and
Leonie de Saint-Vire. Thanks for the inspiration!

CHAPTER ONE

THE LAST THING Cristiano Velazquez—current duke of an ancient and largely forgotten dukedom in Spain, not to mention playboy extraordinaire—wanted to see at two in the morning as he rolled out of his favourite Paris club was a gang of youths crouched in front of his limo as it waited by the kerb. He wanted to hear the distinctive rattle and then hiss of a spray can even less.

God only knew where his driver André was, the lazy *bastardo*, but he certainly wasn't here, guarding his limo like he should have been.

The two women on Cristiano's arm made fearful noises, murmuring fretfully about bodyguards, but Cristiano had never been bothered with protection and he couldn't be bothered now. Quite frankly, some nights he could use the excitement of a mugging, and at least the presence of a gang of Parisian street kids was something out of the ordinary.

Although it would have been better if they hadn't been spray-painting his limo, of course.

Still, the youths were clearly bothering his lady-friends, and if he wanted to spend the rest of the night with both of them in his bed—which he fully intended to do—then he was going to have to handle the situation.

'Allow me, ladies,' he murmured, and strolled unhurriedly towards the assembled youths.

One of them must have seen him, because the kid said something sharp to the rest of his friends and abruptly they all scattered like a pack of wild dogs.

Except for the boy with the spray can, currently graffitiing a rude phrase across the passenger door.

The kid was crouched down, his slight frame swamped by a pair of dirty black jeans and a huge black hoodie with the hood drawn up. He didn't seem to notice Cristiano's approach, absorbed as he was in adding a final flourish to his artwork.

Cristiano paused behind him, admiring said 'artwork'. 'Very good. But you missed an "e",' he pointed out helpfully.

Instantly the kid sprang up from his crouch, throwing the spray can to the right and darting to the left.

But Cristiano was ready for him. He grabbed the back of the boy's hoodie before the kid could escape and held on.

The boy was pulled up short, the hoodie slipping off his head. He made a grab for it, trying to pull it back up, but it was too late. A strand of bright hair escaped, the same pinky-red as apricots.

Cristiano froze. Unusual colour. Familiar in some way.

An old and forgotten memory stirred, and before he knew what he was doing he'd grabbed the boy's narrow shoulders and spun him around, jerking his hood down at the same time.

A wealth of apricot-coloured hair tumbled down the boy's back, framing a pale face with small, finely carved features and big eyes the deep violet-blue of cornflowers.

Not a boy. A girl.

No, a woman.

She said something foul in a voice completely at odds with the air of wide-eyed innocence she projected. A voice made for sex, husky and sweet, that went straight to his groin.

Not a problem. Everything went straight to his groin.

The grip he had on the back of her hoodie tightened.

She spat another curse at him and tried to wriggle out of his hold like a furious kitten.

Cristiano merely tightened his grip, studying her. She was quite strong for a little thing, not to mention feisty, and he really should let her go. Especially when he had other female company standing around behind him. Female company he actually wanted to spend time with tonight.

Then again, that familiarity was nagging at him, tugging at him as insistently as the girl was doing right now. That hair was familiar, and so were those eyes. And that lush little mouth...

Had he seen her before somewhere?

Had he slept with her, maybe?

But, no, surely not. She was dressed in dirty, baggy streetwear, and there was a feral, hungry look to her. He'd been in many dives around the world, and he recognised the look of a person who lived nowhere but the streets, and this young woman had that look.

She had the foul mouth that went along with it, too.

Not that he minded cursing. What he did mind was people spray-painting his limo and interrupting his evening.

'Be still, *gatita*,' he ordered. 'Or I'll call the police.'

At the mention of police she struggled harder, producing a knife from somewhere and waving it threateningly at him.

'Let me go!' she said, and added something rude to do with a very masculine part of his anatomy.

Definitely feisty, and probably more trouble than she was worth—especially with that knife waving around. She was pretty, but he wasn't into expending effort on a woman who was resistant when he had plenty of willing ones who weren't.

Then again, his tastes were…eclectic, and he liked difference. She was certainly that. A bit on the young side, though.

'No,' he said calmly. 'Your customisation of my car I could have ignored. But you have interrupted my evening and scared my friends, and that I simply won't stand for.'

She ignored him, spitting another curse and slashing at him with her knife.

'And now we're dealing with assault,' Cristiano pointed out, not at all bothered by the knife, since it managed to miss him by miles.

'Yes,' she snapped. 'You assaulting me!'

He sighed. He didn't have a lot of patience for this kind of nonsense and now, since it was late—or early, depending on your point of reference—he wanted to get to bed, and not alone. He really needed to handle this unfortunate situation.

So let her go.

Well, he should. After he'd figured out why she was so familiar, because it was really starting to annoy him now.

Though that was going to be difficult with her still swinging wildly at him with a knife.

Amongst the many skills he'd become proficient in on his quest to fill the gaping emptiness inside him was a certain expertise in a couple of martial arts, so it wasn't difficult for him to disarm her of her knife and then bundle her into his limo.

He got in after her and shut the door, locking it for good measure so that she was effectively confined.

Instantly she tried to get out, trying to get the doors to open. It wouldn't work. Only he could open the doors from the inside when they were locked.

He said nothing, watching her as she tried futilely to escape. When it became clear to her that she couldn't, she turned to him, a mix of fury and fear in her big cornflower-blue eyes.

'Let me out,' she demanded, breathless.

Cristiano leaned back in the seat opposite her and shoved his hands into the pockets of his expertly tailored black dress pants. It might have been a stupid move, since it wasn't clear whether she had another knife on her somewhere, but he was betting she didn't.

'No,' he said, studying her face.

Her jaw went rigid, her small figure stiff with tension. 'Are you going to rape me?'

He blinked at the stark question, then had a brief internal debate about whether he should be annoyed she'd even had to ask—especially since the latter part of his life had largely been spent in the pursuit of pleasure, both his own and that of any partners he came into contact with.

But in the end it wasn't worth getting uptight about. If she was indeed on the streets, then not being assaulted was likely to be one of her first concerns.

Particularly when she'd been bundled into a car and locked in by a man much larger and stronger than she was.

'No,' he said flatly, so there could be no doubt. 'That sounds like effort, and I try not to make any effort if I can possibly help it.'

She gazed at him suspiciously. 'Then why did you shut me in this car?'

'Because you tried to stab me with your knife.'

'You could have just let me go.'

'You were graffitiing my car. And it's an expensive car. It's going to cost me a lot of money to get it repainted.'

She gave him a look that was at once disdainful and pitying. 'You can afford it, rich man.'

Unoffended, Cristiano tilted his head, studying her. 'It's true. I am rich. And, yes, I can afford to get it repainted. But it's inconvenient to have to do so. You have inconvenienced me, *gatita*, and I do so hate to be inconvenienced. So, tell me, what are you going to do about it?'

'I'm not going to do anything about it.' She lifted her chin stubbornly. 'Let me out, *fils de pute*.'

'Such language,' Cristiano reproved, entertained despite himself. 'Where did you learn your manners?'

'I'll call the police myself. Tell them you're holding me against my will.'

She dug into the voluminous pockets of her hoodie, brought out a battered-looking cellphone and held it up triumphantly. 'Ten seconds to let me out and then I'm calling the emergency services.'

Cristiano was unmoved. 'Go ahead. I know the police quite well. I'm sure you'll be able to explain why you were crouching in front of my car, spray-painting foul language all over it, and then pulling a knife on me when I tried to stop you.'

She opened her mouth. Closed it again.

'What's your name?' he went on. That nagging familiarity was still tugging at him. He'd seen her before—he was sure of it.

'None of your business.'

Clearly she'd thought better of calling the police, because she lowered her hand disappearing her phone back into her hoodie.

'Give me back my knife.'

Cristiano was amused. She was a brave little *gatita*, asking for the knife he'd only just disarmed her of after she'd tried to stab him with it. Brave to stand up to him, too—especially considering she was at a severe disadvantage. Not only physically but, given her dirty clothes and feral air, socially, too.

Then again, when you lived at the bottom of life's barrel you had nothing to left to lose. He knew. He'd been there himself—if not physically then certainly in spirit.

'Sadly, that's not going to happen.' He shifted, taking his hands out of his pockets and very slowly leaning forward, his elbows on his thighs, his fingers linked loosely between his knees.

A wary look crossed her face.

And that was good. She was right to be wary. Because he was losing his patience, and when he lost patience he was dangerous. Very dangerous indeed.

'I'll ask one more time,' he said, letting a warning edge his voice. 'What's your name, *gatita*?'

The man sitting opposite Leonie—the rich bastard who'd scooped her up and put her in his limo—was scaring the living daylights out of her, and she wasn't sure why.

He wasn't being threatening. He was simply sitting there with his hands between his knees, eyes the same kind of green as deep, dense jungles staring unblinkingly at her.

He was dressed all in black, and she didn't need to be rich to know that his clothes—black trousers and a plain black cotton shirt—had been made for him. Nothing else explained the way they fitted him so perfectly, framing wide shoulders and a broad chest, a lean waist and powerful thighs.

He reeked of money, this man. She could virtually smell it.

And not just money. He reeked of power, too. It was an almost physical force, pushing at her, crowding out all the air in the car and winding long fingers around her throat and squeezing.

There was another element to that power, though. An element she couldn't identify.

It had something to do with his face, which was as

beautiful as some of the carved angels on the tombs in the Père Lachaise Cemetery. Yet that wasn't quite it. He seemed warmer than an angel, so maybe more like a fallen one. Maybe a beautiful devil instead.

Night-black hair, straight brows and those intense green eyes…

No, he wasn't an angel, and he wasn't a devil, either. He seemed more vital than a mythical being. More…elemental, somehow.

He was a black panther in the jungle, watching her from the branch of a tree. All sleepy and lazy… Until he was ready to pounce.

That frightened her—but it didn't feel like a threat she was familiar with. Sleeping on the streets of Paris had given her a very acute sense of threat, especially the threat of physical violence, and she wasn't getting that from him.

No, it was something else.

'Why do you want to know my name?'

She wasn't going to just give it to him. She never gave her name to anyone unless she knew them. Over the past few years she'd developed a hearty distrust of most people and it had saved her on more than one occasion.

'So you can call your friends in the police and get them to throw me in jail?'

She shouldn't have vandalised the car, since as a rule she liked to keep a low profile—less chance of coming to anyone's notice that way. But she'd been followed on her way to the little alley where she'd been hoping to bed down and, since being a woman on her own at night could be a problem, she'd attached herself to the crowd of homeless teenagers she'd been with earlier. They'd been out vandalising stuff and she'd had to prove herself willing to do the same in order to stay in their company. So she hadn't hesitated to pick up the spray can.

To be fair, she hadn't minded targeting this man's limo. The rich never saw the people on the streets, and she rather liked the idea of forcing her existence to at least be acknowledged in some way. Even if it did involve the police.

'No.'

His voice was very deep, with a warmth curling through it that made a part of her shiver right down low inside. There was a lilt to it, too…a faint, musical accent.

'But you were vandalising my car. Your name is the least you can give me in recompense.'

Leonie frowned. What had he done with her knife? She wanted it back. She didn't feel safe without it. 'Why? Don't you want money?'

He raised one perfect black brow. 'Do you have any?'

'No.'

The man shrugged one powerful shoulder in an elegant motion and she found her gaze drawn by the movement. To the way his shirt pulled tight across that shoulder, displaying the power of the muscles underneath.

How odd. She'd never looked at a man that way before, so why was she doing so now? Men were awful—especially rich men like this one. She knew all about them; her father was one of them and he'd thrown her and her mother out on the streets. So no wonder she'd taken an instant dislike to this guy—though maybe it was more hate than dislike.

Hate was the only word strong enough to describe the disturbingly intense feeling gathering inside her now.

'Then, *gatita*,' he said, in his dark, deep voice, 'your name it will have to be.'

'But I don't want to give you that.'

Her jaw tightened. Resistance was the only thing she had on the streets and she clung to it stubbornly. Resistance to anything and everything that tried to push her down or squash her, grind her into the dirt of Paris's ancient cobbles. Because if she didn't resist then what else did she have? How would she even know she existed?

By spraying rude words on a limo?

Yes, if need be. It was all about the fight. That was all life was.

He gave another elegant shrug, as if it was all out of his hands. 'Then sadly I must be recompensed for my inconvenience in other ways.'

Ah, of course. She understood this, at least. 'I'm not paying you in sex. I'd rather die.'

His mouth twitched, which she found disconcerting. Normally men got angry when she refused them, but he didn't seem angry at all. Only…amused.

For some reason she didn't like it that he found her amusing.

'I'm sure you wouldn't,' he said lazily. 'I happen to be very good at it. No one has died having sex with me yet, for example.'

Leonie ignored the way her stomach fluttered. Perhaps that was hunger. She hadn't eaten today, and although a day without food was fairly normal for her, she didn't usually find herself chucked into a limo and kept prisoner by…whoever this man was.

'But,' he went on before she could argue, 'I know what you're talking about, and rest assured my recompense won't be in the form of sex. Though I'm sure you are, in fact, very desirable.'

She gave him a dark look. 'I am, actually. Why do you think I carry a knife?'

'Of course. What man wouldn't want a feral kitten?'

His mouth curved and she found herself staring at it. It had a nice shape, firm and beautifully carved.

She shook herself. Why was she staring at his mouth?

'You'd be surprised what men want,' she said, dragging her gaze to meet his, though quite frankly that wasn't any better.

His amusement abruptly drained away, the lines of his perfect face hardening. He shifted, sitting back against the seat. 'No. I would not.'

Leonie shivered, the interior of the car feeling suddenly cold. 'What do you want, then? I can't pay you, and I'm not telling you my name, so all you can do is call the police and have me prosecuted. And if you're not going to do that, then isn't it easier to let me go?'

'But then how would I be recompensed for my inconvenience?' He shook his head slowly. 'No, I'm afraid, *gatita*, I can't let you go.' He paused, his green eyes considering. 'I think I'm going to have to put you to work instead.'

CHAPTER TWO

THE LITTLE REDHEAD treated this suggestion without obvious enthusiasm—which Cristiano had expected.

He still didn't know why exactly he'd said it. Because she was right. He could afford the paltry amount it would take to get his limo repainted. And as for his supposed inconvenience…

He glanced out through the window to the two lovely women he'd wanted to join him for the night. They were still out there, waiting for him to give them the word, though for once he felt a lessening of his own enthusiasm for their company.

It was a bit mystifying, since he never said no to anything or anyone—still less two beautiful women. Nevertheless, he found himself more interested in the little *gatita* sitting opposite him. She was a puzzle, and it had been too long since he'd had a puzzle.

He wanted her name. And the fact that she wouldn't just give it to him was irritating. Especially when that familiarity kept tugging on him, rubbing against his consciousness like a burr in a blanket.

Women never denied him, and the fact that she had was annoying.

And then she'd muttered that thing about men, and he'd realised that letting her go meant letting her go back on the streets at two in the morning. Admittedly she'd been with a crowd earlier, but they'd all vanished, so she'd be on her own.

That she was used to looking after herself was obvious, but it didn't mean he was going to let her. He wasn't a gentleman, despite the fact that he came from an ancient line of Spanish nobility. Not in any way. But he was enough of a man that he couldn't leave this young woman alone in the middle of the night.

Because, no, he wouldn't be surprised at what men wanted from such a delectable little morsel such as herself. He was one of those men after all.

That left him with only one option: to keep hold of her in a way she'd accept.

He could, of course, simply ignore her protests and take her back to his Paris mansion and keep her there. But, again, dealing with the protests that would no doubt entail would be tiresome, and he preferred to avoid tiresome things. Things that left less time to do the things he liked doing. His own personal pleasure always took priority.

It would be easier all round if she agreed, therefore work it was.

If only he had something for her to do...

He had estates and a *castillo* back in Spain—

which he avoided going to whenever possible—and numerous companies he'd invested his considerable fortune in. But he already had a number of staff managing all those things—and besides, they weren't the kinds of things a Parisian street urchin could manage, no matter how feisty she was.

No, the only work he could conceivably give her was domestic, by adding her to his housekeeping staff. He already had a large contingent, but one more wouldn't hurt. House-cleaning, at least, required no extensive training, and it would keep her close until he'd uncovered her mysteries.

Which he was going to do, since he currently had a dearth of mysteries in his life.

'What kind of work?' she asked, still suspicious.

'I need someone to clean for me.' He tilted his head, studying her. 'I have a house in Paris that's very large and needs attention. You may work out what you owe me for the car and my personal inconvenience there.'

'But I—'

'Did I mention that I have rooms set aside for my staff? You will be required to live on-site for the duration.'

'Don't guys like you already have a lot people doing your dirty work for you?'

'Yes.' Her scorn didn't bother him. He tried not to let anything bother him, since it was very dangerous for all concerned when he was bothered. 'But I could always do with one more. Plus, I pay my staff very well for doing my "dirty work".'

At the mention of pay, something changed. Her eyes lost that wary look, and a calculating gleam sparked in their depths.

He knew that gleam and he knew it intimately. It was hunger. And not in the physical sense, of needing food, but in the sense of wanting something you could never have and wanting it desperately.

Money—she wanted money. And who could blame her when she didn't have any? Money was power, and she didn't have any of that, either, he'd bet.

Sure enough, she said, 'Pay? You pay them?'

'Of course. That's why they're my staff and not my slaves.'

She leaned forward all of a sudden, losing her wariness, all business now. Her violet eyes were focused very intently on him. 'Would you pay me? Once I earned back for the car? Could I have a proper job?'

Something shifted in Cristiano's gut. Something that, again, he was intimately familiar with.

She was lovely. And he could imagine her looking at him just like that, with a pretty flush to her pale cheeks and a flame in her eyes and all the beautiful hair spread over his pillow. Hungry for him as he buried himself inside her...

A nice thought, but a thought was what it would stay. She'd never be one of his partners. Apart from the fact that the distance between them in power, money and just about everything else could not have been more vast, she was also much younger than he was.

And he was betting she'd either had some bad experiences with men or she avoided men completely.

Again, dealing with all that sounded like work, and he tried to avoid work whenever he could. He didn't want anything hard, anything difficult, and he avoided complications like the plague.

This small *gatita* was certainly a complication, but he found he was willing to expend a bit of effort on figuring out why she was so familiar to him. After all, it had been a while since he'd let himself be interested in something other than physical pleasure. It certainly couldn't hurt.

'Do you want a job?' he asked, teasing her a little just because he could.

'Yes, of course I want a job.' Her gaze narrowed further. 'How much do you pay?'

A good question—though he was sure she couldn't afford to turn anything down.

'My staff are the best and I pay them accordingly,' he said, and named a sum that made her pretty eyes go round.

'That much?' All her earlier wariness and suspicion had dropped away. 'You really pay people that much just to clean your house?'

'It's a very big house.'

'And you'd pay me that?'

It wasn't a lot of money—at least it wasn't to him. But for her it was clearly a fortune. Then again, he suspected that a five-euro note left on the street would be a fortune for her.

'Yes, I'd pay you that.' He paused, studying her. 'Where do you live? And what are you doing on the streets at two in the morning?'

Instantly her expression closed up, the light disappearing from her face, the shutters coming down behind her eyes. She sat back on the seat, putting distance between them and glancing out of the window.

'I should go home. My…mother will be worried.'

Which didn't answer his direct question but answered the ones he hadn't voiced. Because she was lying. Her slight hesitation made him pretty certain she didn't have a mother and neither did she have a home.

'I think not,' he said, watching her. 'I think you should come directly back to my house and spend the night there. Then you can start work first thing tomorrow morning.'

'I don't want to come back to your house.'

'Like I said, I have quarters for my staff and there will be more than enough room.'

'But I—'

'There will be no argument.' Because he'd decided now, and once he made a decision he stuck to it. 'You have two choices. Either you come back to my house tonight or you spend the night in a police cell.'

'That's not much of a choice,' she said angrily.

'Too bad. You were the one who decided spray-painting my car was a good idea, so these are the consequences.' He liked her arguing with him, he realised. Probably too much—which was an issue. 'So what's it to be, *gatita*?'

She folded her arms. 'Why do you keep calling me that?'

'It means kitten in Spanish.'

'I'm not a kitten.'

'You're small and feral and you tried to scratch me—of course you're a kitten. And a wild one at that.'

She was silent a moment, not at all mollified. Then, 'Why Spanish?'

'Because I'm Spanish.'

'Oh. What are you doing in Paris?'

He stared at her, letting her see a little of his edge. 'That's a lot of questions for a woman who won't even give me her name.'

'Why should I? You haven't given me yours.'

That was true—he hadn't. And why not? His name was an ancient and illustrious one, but one that would soon come to an end. He was the sole heir and he had no plans to produce another. No, the Velazquez line, the dukedom of San Lorenzo, would die with him and then be forgotten. Which was probably for the best, considering his dissolute lifestyle.

Your parents would be appalled.

They certainly would have been had they still been alive, but they weren't. He had no one to impress, no one to live up to. There was only him and he didn't care.

'My name is Cristiano Velazquez, Fifteenth Duke of San Lorenzo,' he said, because he had no reason to hide it. 'And you may address me as Your Grace.'

A ripple of something crossed her face, though he couldn't tell what it was. Then she frowned. 'A duke? Cristiano Velazquez…?' She said his name very slowly, as if tasting it.

He knew she hadn't meant to do it in a seductive way, but he felt the seduction in it all the same. His name in her soft, sweet husky voice, said so carefully in French… As if that same sense of familiarity tugged at her the way it tugged at him.

But how would she know him? They'd never met—or at least not that he remembered. And he definitely hadn't slept with her—that he was sure of. He might have had too many women to count, but he'd remember if he'd had her.

'You've heard of me?' he asked carefully, watching her face.

'No… I don't think so.' She looked away. 'Where is your house, then?'

Was she telling the truth? Had she, in fact, heard of him? Briefly he debated whether or not to push her. But it was late, and there were dark circles under her eyes, and suddenly she looked very small and fragile sitting there.

He should get her back to his place and tuck her into bed.

'You'll see.' Moving over the seat towards the door, he opened it. 'Stay here.'

Not that he gave her much choice, because he got out and shut it behind him again, locking it just in case she decided to make a desperate bid for freedom.

He made excuses to the two patiently waiting women, ensured they were taken care of for the evening, then went to find his recalcitrant driver, whom he eventually found in a nearby alley, playing some kind of dice game with a couple of the kids who'd been standing around his car.

How fortunate.

Getting his wallet out of his pocket, Cristiano extracted a note and brandished it at one of the youths. 'You,' he said shortly. 'This is yours if you tell me the name of the woman with the pretty red hair who was spray-painting my car.'

The kid stared at the note, his mouth open. 'Uh… Leonie,' he muttered, and made a grab for the money.

So much for loyalty.

Cristiano jerked the note away before the boy could get it. 'You didn't give me a last name.'

The kid scowled. 'I don't know. No one knows anyone's last name around here.'

Which was probably true.

He allowed the boy to take the money and then, with a meaningful jerk of his head towards the car for his driver's benefit, he turned back to it himself.

Leonie. Leonie…

Somewhere in the dim recesses of his memory a bell rang.

Leonie blinked as a pair of big wrought-iron gates set into a tall stone wall opened and the car slid smoothly through them.

On the rare occasions when she'd ventured out of the area she lived in she'd seen places like this. Old buildings surrounded by high walls. Houses where the rich lived.

She'd once lived in a house like this herself, but it had been a long time ago and elsewhere, when she'd been a little kid. Before her father had kicked her and her mother out of their palatial mansion and life had changed drastically.

She still remembered what it had been like to have money, to have a roof over her head and clean clothes and food. Nice memories, but they'd been a lie, so she tried not to think about them. It was better not to remember such things because they only made her want what she could never have—and wanting things was always a bad thing.

She stared distrustfully out into the darkness, where the silhouette of a massive old house reared against the sky.

The driver came around the side of the car and opened the door. The duke gestured at her to get out.

She turned her distrustful attention to him.

A duke. An honest-to-God duke. He didn't look

like one—though she had no idea what dukes were supposed to look like. Maybe much older. Although, given the faint lines around his eyes and mouth, he was certainly a lot older than she was. Then again, his hair was still pitch-black so he couldn't be *that* old.

His name had sounded faintly familiar to her, though she couldn't think why. The fact that he was Spanish had given her a little kick, since she'd been born in Spain herself. In fact maybe she'd met him once before—back in Spain, before her father had got rid of her and her mother and her mother had dragged her to Paris.

Back when she'd been Leonie de Riero, the prized only daughter of Victor de Riero, with the blood of ancient Spanish aristocracy running in her veins.

Perhaps she knew this duke from then? Or perhaps not. She'd been very young, after all, and her memories of that time were dim.

Whatever he was, or had been, she didn't want to remember those days. The present was the only thing she had, and she had to be on her guard at all times. Forgetting where she was and what was happening led to mistakes, and she'd already made enough of those since ending up on the streets.

If she hadn't been so absorbed in getting the lettering just so as she'd graffitied his car, she wouldn't be here after all.

You certainly wouldn't have had a bed for the night, so maybe it wasn't such a mistake?

That remained to be seen. Perhaps she should have

fought harder to escape him. Then again, she hadn't been able to resist the lure of a job—if he actually meant what he'd said, that was.

The duke lifted that perfect brow of his. 'Are you going to get out? Or would you prefer to sit here all night? The car is quite comfortable, though I'm afraid the doors will have to stay locked.'

She gave him a ferocious glare. 'Give me back my knife first.' She liked to have some protection on her, just in case of treachery.

He remained impervious to her glare. 'I'm not going to hurt you, *gatita*.'

Kitten. He kept calling her kitten. It was annoying.

'I don't trust you. And I don't want to sleep in a strange place without some protection.'

His jungle-green gaze was very level and absolutely expressionless. 'Fair enough.' Reaching into the pocket of his jacket, he extracted her knife and held it out, handle first.

She took it from him, the familiarity of the handle fitting into her palm making her feel slightly better. Briefly she debated whether or not to try and slash at him again, then bolt into the darkness. But she remembered the high walls surrounding the house. She wouldn't be able to get over those, alas. She could refuse to get out and sleep in the car, but she didn't like the idea of being locked in. No, it was the house or nothing.

With as much dignity as she could muster, Leonie pocketed her knife then slid out of the car. Behind her, the duke murmured something to his driver and then he was beside her, moving past her up the big stone steps to the front door of the mansion.

Some member of his staff was obviously still up, because the door opened, a pool of light shining out.

A minute later she found herself in a huge vaulted vestibule, with flights of stone steps curling up to the upper storeys and a massive, glittering chandelier lighting the echoing space. Thick silk rugs lay on the floor and there were pictures on the walls, and on the ceiling far above her head was a big painting of angels with white wings and golden haloes.

It was very warm inside.

She was used to being cold. She'd been cold ever since she was sixteen, coming home after school one day to the rundown apartment she'd shared with her mother only to find it empty, and a note from her mother on the rickety kitchen table informing Leonie that she'd gone and not to look for her.

Leonie hadn't believed it at first. But her mother hadn't come home that night, or the next, or the one after that, and eventually Leonie had had to accept that her mother wasn't coming home at all. Leonie had been evicted from the apartment not long after that, and forced to live on the streets, where she'd felt like she'd become permanently cold.

But she hadn't realised just how cold until now. Until the warmth from this place seeped up through the cracked soles of her sneakers and into her body, into her heart.

Immediately she wanted to go outside again—to run and never stop running. She couldn't trust this warmth. She couldn't let her guard down. It wasn't safe.

Except the big front door had closed, and she knew it would be locked, and the duke was gesturing at her to follow the older woman who stood next to him, regarding her with some disgust, making her abruptly conscious of the holes in her jeans and the stains on the denim. Of the grimy hoodie that she'd stolen from a guy who'd taken it off to fight someone in the alleyway where she'd been sleeping one night. Of the paint stains on her hands.

She was dirty, and ragged, and she probably smelled since she hadn't found anywhere to clean herself for weeks. No wonder this woman looked disgusted.

Leonie's stomach clenched and she gripped the handle of her knife, scowling to cover the wave of vulnerability that had come over her. Never stop fighting. Never show weakness. That was the law of the streets.

'Go with Camille,' the duke said. 'She will show you—'

'No,' Leonie said. 'Just tell me where to go and I'll find my own way there.'

Camille made a disapproving sound, then said something in a lilting musical language to the duke. He replied in the same language, his deep, rich voice making it sound as if he was caressing each word.

Leonie felt every one of her muscles tense in resistance. She couldn't like the sound of his voice. She had to be on her guard at all times and not make any mistakes. And she didn't want to go with this Camille woman and her disapproving stare.

Much to her surprise, however, with one last dark look in Leonie's direction, the woman turned and vanished down one of the huge, echoing hallways that led off the entrance hall.

Without a word, the duke turned and headed towards the huge marble staircase. 'Follow me,' he said over his shoulder.

He didn't pause and he didn't wait, as if expecting her to follow him just as he'd said.

Leonie blinked. Why had he sent the other woman away? Was he just leaving her here? What if she somehow managed to get out through the door? What if she escaped down one of the corridors? What would he do? He wasn't looking at her. Would he even know until she was gone?

Her heartbeat thumped wildly, adrenaline surging through her—both preludes to a very good bolt. And yet she wasn't moving. She was standing there in this overwhelming, intimidating entrance hall, not running, watching a tall, powerful rich man go up the marble stairs.

He moved with economy and a lazy, athletic grace that reminded her even more strongly of a panther. It was mesmerising, for some reason. And when she found herself moving, it wasn't towards the doorway or the corridor, it was towards him, following him almost helplessly.

Was this what had happened in that fairy-tale? Those children following the Pied Piper, drawn beyond their control by the music he made. Disappearing. Never to be seen again.

You're an idiot. You have your knife. Pull yourself together.

This was true. And nothing had happened to her so far. Yes, he'd kept her locked in the car against her will, but he hadn't hurt her. And apart from the moment when he'd grabbed her, he hadn't touched her again.

She didn't trust him, or his offer of a job, but it was either follow him or stay down here in the entrance hall, and that seemed cowardly. She wasn't going to do that, either.

There was a slim possibility that he was telling the truth, and if so she needed to take advantage of it. If she was going to achieve her dream of having a little cottage of her own in the countryside, away from the city, away from danger, then he was her best chance of that happening.

Slowly Leonie moved after him, going up the winding marble staircase, trying to keep her attention on his strong back and not gawk at all the paintings on the walls, the carpets on the parquet floors, the vases of flowers on the small tables dotted here and there as they went down yet another wide and high-ceilinged corridor.

Windows let in the Parisian night and she caught glimpses of tall trees, hinting at a garden outside. She wanted to go and look through the glass, because it had been a long time since she'd seen a garden, but she didn't dare. She had to keep the duke's tall figure in sight.

Eventually, after leading her through a few more of those high-ceilinged corridors, he stopped outside a door and opened it, inclining his head for her to go on through.

He was standing quite near the doorway, and she wasn't sure she wanted to get that close to him, but she didn't want him to know it bothered her, either, so she slipped past him as quickly as she could. But not quickly enough to avoid catching a hint of his aftershave and the warmth of his powerful body as she brushed past him.

It was only an instant, but in that instant she was acutely aware of his height looming over her. Of the width of his broad shoulders and the stretch of the cotton across his muscled chest. Of the way he smelled spicy and warm and quite delicious.

A strange ripple of sensation went through her like an electric shock.

Disturbed, Leonie ignored it, concentrating instead on the room she'd stepped into.

It was very large, with tall windows that looked out on to trees. A thick pale carpet covered the floor, and up against one wall, facing the windows, was a very large bed, made up with a thick, soft-looking white quilt.

The duke moved past her, going over to the windows and drawing heavy pale silk curtains over the black glass, shutting out the night. The room was very warm, the carpet very soft under her feet, and she was conscious once again of how dirty she was.

She was going to leave stains all over this pretty pale bedroom. Surely he couldn't mean for her to stay here? It didn't look like a cleaner's room. It was far too luxurious.

'This can't be where you put your staff,' she said, frowning. 'Why am I here?'

He adjusted the curtains with a small, precise movement, then turned around, putting his hands in his pockets. 'Not usually, no. But Camille didn't have a room ready for you, so I thought you could use one of my guest bedrooms.'

'Why? Why are you doing this?'

He tilted his head, gazing at her from underneath very long, thick black lashes. 'Which particular "this" are you talking about?'

'I mean this room. A job. A bed for the night. Why are you doing any of it? Why should you care?'

She hadn't meant it to come out so accusingly, but she couldn't help it. Men like him, with money and power, never did things without wanting something in return. Even charity usually came with strings. There were bound to be strings here, if only she could see them.

But the duke merely gave one of those elegant shrugs. 'What else does one do with a feral kitten but look after it?'

'I'm not a kitten,' she said, for the second time that night.

His mouth curved and once again she felt that electric ripple of sensation move through her. It came to her very suddenly that this man was dangerous. And dangerous in a way she couldn't name. He wasn't a physical threat—though those strange little ripples of sensation definitely were—but definitely a threat of some kind.

'No,' he murmured, his gaze moving over her in a way that made heat rise in her cheeks. 'You're not, are you?'

She lifted her chin, discomfited and not liking it one bit. 'And I didn't ask you to look after me, either.'

'Oh, if you think I'm doing it out of the goodness of my heart you are mistaken.' He strolled past her towards the door. 'It's entirely out of self-interest, believe me.'

'Why? Just because I vandalised your car?'

Pausing by the door, he gave her a sweeping, enigmatic glance. 'Among other things. The bathroom is through the door opposite. A shower or a bath wouldn't go amiss, *gatita*.'

'Don't call me that,' she snapped, annoyed that he'd obviously noticed how dirty she was and how she must smell, and then annoyed further by her own annoyance—since why should she care if he'd noticed?

'What else am I to call you?' His eyes gleamed. 'Especially since you won't give me your name.'

Leonie pressed her lips together. He might have strong-armed her into staying in his house, but her name was the one thing he wouldn't be able to force out of her. That was hers to give.

Again, he didn't seem offended. He only smiled. 'Then *gatita* it will have to be.'

And before she could say another word he walked out, closing the door carefully behind him.

CHAPTER THREE

THE LATE-MORNING SUN poured through the big windows of Cristiano's study, flooding the room with light and warmth, but he didn't notice. He wasn't interested in the weather.

He'd got up early that morning, despite not having slept much the previous night, and gone straight to his study to see if the memory that learning Leonie's name had generated was correct. After a couple of calls and a few strongly worded orders he'd had his confirmation.

She was exactly who he'd suspected she was.

Which should have been impossible, considering she was supposed to be dead.

He leaned back in his big black leather chair and stared at the computer screen on the desk in front of him. At the photo it displayed. An old one, from years and years ago, of a tall, dark-haired man, holding the hand of a little girl with hair the distinctive colour of apricots. At the side of the little girl stood a lovely slender woman with hair exactly the same colour.

It was a loving family portrait of the ancient and illustrious de Riero family—Spanish aristocrats who'd fallen on hard times and lost their title a century or so ago.

Leonie had turned out to be Leonie de Riero, Victor de Riero's prized only daughter, who'd disappeared along with her mother fifteen years earlier, rumoured to have died in an apartment fire in Barcelona not long after she'd disappeared.

It was a scandal that had rocked Spain for months and he remembered it acutely. Especially because Victor de Riero, whose family had been blood enemies of Cristiano's, had become his mentor.

Victor had been grief-stricken about the loss of his wife and child—at least until he'd found himself a new family.

Your family.

The deep, volcanic rage that Cristiano had thought he'd excised from his life shifted in his gut, hot enough to incinerate anything in its path, and he had to take a minute to wrestle it back into submission. Because he couldn't allow himself to feel that—not any more. He couldn't allow himself to feel anything any more.

It had taken him years to put that rage behind him, but he had. And he'd thought he'd found some measure of peace. Until Leonie had appeared.

Cristiano pushed his chair back and got to his feet, walking over to the bookshelves opposite his desk before turning and pacing back to the desk again, needing movement to settle himself.

His thoughts tumbled about in his head like dice.

Of course Leonie had been familiar to him. He *had* met her. But it had been years ago, and she'd been that little girl in the photo—a kid of around two or three, initially, when her father had first approached him.

He'd been seventeen at the time, and had just lost both his parents in a car accident. Victor de Riero had paid him a visit not long after the funeral, ostensibly to bury the hatchet on the ancient feud the Velazquez and de Riero families had been pursuing for centuries.

Cristiano had been only too happy to do so, having no interest in old feuds and still grappling with the deaths of his parents and the shock of suddenly having to take on the responsibility of a dukedom. He'd welcomed Victor's interest in him gratefully, listening to the older man's advice and accepting his help, thinking the other man was doing it out of the goodness of his heart.

But he hadn't known then that there was no goodness in Victor's heart, or that the flames of vengeance for the de Riero family still burned in him hot and strong.

In fact it hadn't been until Cristiano had married, three years later, that he'd discovered the truth about Victor de Riero's interest.

In that time, though, he'd met Victor's wife and

his small, sparky daughter. Cristiano hadn't taken much notice of the daughter—kids hadn't been on his radar back then—but then Victor's wife had disappeared, taking the girl with her, only for both to be discovered dead in a fire a week or so later.

Cristiano had tried to be there for Victor the way Victor had been for him, after his parents had died, but he'd been in the throes of first love, and then early marriage, and hadn't paid as much attention as he should have.

He hadn't paid attention a year or so after that, either, when he'd gone to Victor for advice when his marriage to Anna had run into trouble. If he had, he might have noticed how much his wife had enjoyed Victor's company—how, at social occasions, she'd spent more time talking to him than she had to Cristiano.

He might have become aware that Victor had never planned on burying the hatchet when it came to their family feud but had only been lying in wait, lulling Cristiano into a false sense of security, waiting for the right time to take advantage of a vulnerable young man.

And finally he had found that advantage in Cristiano's wife. Because it had been his lovely wife Anna that Victor had wanted, and in the end it had been his lovely wife that he'd taken—Cristiano's already pregnant wife.

Along with Cristiano's son.

Cristiano paced to the bookshelves again, memories he'd long since suppressed flooding like acid through him.

Victor turning up at Cristiano's Barcelona penthouse, flanked by bodyguards and cloaked in triumph, revealing the final piece of his plot like a pantomime villain. Rubbing salt into Cristiano's wound by telling him that his seduction of Anna had all been part of their blood feud, and then rubbing glass into that same wound by telling him that Anna was pregnant and the child was Cristiano's.

He would bring up Cristiano's child as his own, Victor had said. He would take something precious from a Velazquez after a Velazquez had ruined the de Riero family a century earlier, by stealing the dukedom from them.

Cristiano had barely heard the man's reasoning. He'd been incandescent with rage and betrayal. It had been wise of Victor to have brought bodyguards, because he hadn't been at all sure he wouldn't have launched himself at the other man and strangled him.

Your anger has always been a problem.

Yes, and he'd been on fire with it.

For two years he'd used almost the entirety of his fortune trying to get his son back, but Victor had falsified the paternity tests Cristiano had demanded, paid any number of people off, and Cristiano hadn't had a leg to stand on.

Eventually he'd crashed a party of Victor's, intent on stealing back his son from the man who'd taken him—but when he'd approached the boy, the child had run from him in fear. Straight to Victor.

'This is the reason, Cristiano,' Anna had flung at him, as she'd tried to calm the hysterical child in Victor's arms. *'This is the reason I left you. You're dangerous and you only end up scaring people. Why can't you leave us alone?'*

Well, she'd got her wish in the end. After that— after seeing the fear in his son's green eyes—he'd left the party. Left Spain, vowing never to return.

For his own sanity he'd excised all knowledge of his son from his heart, scoured all thoughts of revenge from his soul. He had found other ways to kill the pain lodged inside him like a jagged shard of broken glass. Pleasure and lots of it had been the key, and soon enough the edges of that piece of glass had dulled, making him look back over the years and marvel at how it had ever been sharp enough to hurt.

But it was hurting now. Because of her.

He came to the bookshelves and turned around, pacing back to the desk once more.

If he'd had any sense he'd have got rid of her the moment that sense of nagging familiarity had hit him, but he hadn't, and now she was here. In his house. And he was certain it was her.

A member of his staff had managed to track down the man who'd told Victor that Leonie and Hélène de Riero had died in a fire, and the man— once some money had been waved in his face—had admitted he'd lied. That Hélène de Riero had paid him to report her and her daughter's death to her ex-husband for reasons unknown.

Of course Cristiano would need DNA confirmation, which he'd get easily enough, but he was sure already. No other woman he'd ever met had had hair that colour or those jewel-bright violet eyes.

He had Victor de Riero's daughter in his grasp.

Tension gathered inside him and a vicious anticipation twisted through it, the rage he'd never been able to conquer entirely burning in his heart. Whether it was fate that had brought her to his door, or merely simple chance, it didn't matter.

What mattered was that here was an opportunity. A very unexpected opportunity.

Isn't revenge a dish best served cold?

After his parents had been killed, the old family feud with the de Rieros had seemed like something out of the Middle Ages. A hold-over from a different time. But he'd been young back then, and naive. He hadn't yet learned that people lied and that they couldn't be trusted. He hadn't yet learned just how far the depths of grief and loss could go.

He'd learned eventually. Oh, yes, he'd learned that lesson well.

And now here was his chance to pay that lesson back in kind.

Tension crawled through him, making his jaw ache as he came to the desk and turned around to the bookshelf again.

He couldn't deny that he liked the thought. Relished it.

Victor de Riero had taken his son, so wouldn't it be the sweetest revenge of all if Cristiano took his daughter? The daughter who'd been presumed dead for fifteen years?

An eye for an eye keeps the feud alive.

Perhaps he wouldn't have considered it if Leonie hadn't turned up. Perhaps he'd have gone through his life pretending he didn't have a son and that he'd never been married for the rest of his days. But she had, and now he could think of nothing else.

It seemed the old Spanish warlord in him wasn't as dead as he'd thought.

Maybe he'd make her his duchess. Invite de Riero to the wedding. He'd pull up her veil and then there she'd be—the daughter de Riero had thought was dead, marrying the man he'd once thought he could humiliate in front of the entire world.

And maybe to really pay him back Cristiano would have an heir with her after all. Pollute the pure de Riero bloodline with Velazquez blood.

After all, if de Riero could do it, why couldn't he?

He stopped mid-pace, his fingers curling inside his pockets, vicious pleasure pulling tight in his gut.

And then you can move on.

Not that he hadn't moved on already, but that jagged shard of glass was still embedded deep inside his heart, ensuring it could never heal. Perhaps if he took the revenge he was owed it finally would.

Certainty settled inside him like the earth settling after an earthquake, forming a new landscape.

First on the agenda would be Leonie—because she was vital to his plan and would have to agree to it. Which might be a problem when she was so stubborn, wary and distrustful. Not so surprising, given the circumstances under which he'd found her, but not exactly conducive to his plan. Then again, money seemed to motivate her. She could consider being his bride part of her job, for which she'd receive a very healthy bonus.

Revealing that he knew who she was could be a concern, however. She hadn't given him her name for a reason, and everything hinged on how she felt about her father. Had she ever wanted to return to him? Did she even know she was supposed to be dead?

He frowned at the wall opposite. Perhaps telling her about his discovery immediately would be a mistake. Now she was here, within his grasp, he couldn't afford for her to run, and he'd be at risk of scaring her away if he wasn't careful. No, maybe it would be better to gain her trust before he let her in on his secret—an easy enough task to accomplish with a beautiful woman. All it would require was a bit of careful handling.

Galvanised in a way he hadn't been for years, Cristiano turned towards the door, heading out of his study and going in search of the newest member of his staff.

He found her, as he'd expected, in the big library that faced onto the walled garden at the rear of the house. She was kneeling on the floor before one of the big bookshelves with her back to him. Her dirty clothes were gone—clearly Camille had found her something else to wear—and she now wore the staff uniform of plain black trousers and a fitted black T-shirt. Nondescript clothes that should have made her blend in, and yet the skein of silken hair that fell down her back in a sleek ponytail effectively prevented that. The colour glowed against her black T-shirt, a deep red-gold tinged with pink.

Beautiful.

His hands itched with the urge to run his fingers through it, to see if it felt as soft as it looked. To touch that vibrant colour, wind it round his wrist, examine the contrast against his own skin...

Except that was not what he wanted from her. Her name, yes. Her body, no. He might find her more attractive than he'd expected, but he could get sex from any of the women in his extensive little black book. He didn't need to expend any effort on a skittish, homeless, much younger woman, no matter how pretty her hair was.

But what about your plans for an heir?

Ah, yes, but there would be time for that later.

He hitched one shoulder up against the doorframe and gazed at her.

It was clear she wasn't actually cleaning, since her cloth and polishing spray were sitting next to her. Her head was bent, as if she was looking at something, and it must be very absorbing since it was clear she hadn't heard him and he hadn't exactly been quiet.

That was what had got her into trouble the previous night, hadn't it? She'd been totally caught up in the 'art' she'd been creating on his limo door and hadn't run when she should have.

What would that attention be like it bed? Would she look at you that way? Would she touch you like—?

Cristiano jerked his offending thoughts out of the gutter, irritated with himself. Perhaps he needed to contact those two lovely women he'd been going to take home the previous night and finish what they'd started. Certainly he'd have to do something with his wayward groin—especially if he kept having thoughts like these about Leonie.

He shifted against the doorframe and said finally, 'Find some interesting reading material, *gatita*?'

The duke's deep, rich voice slid over Leonie's skin like an unexpected caress, making her jump in shock, then freeze in place, the book she'd been reading still clutched in her hands. She stared at the shelves in front of her, every sense she had focused on the voice that had come from behind her.

A small cold thread wound its way through her veins.

Her employer had caught her reading on the job on her very first day. Not a good look. Ugh—what had she been thinking?

Everything had been going extremely well since

he'd left her the night before, too. She'd availed herself of the shower, even though everything in her had
wanted to spend hours soaking in the vast white marble bath. But it had been very late and she'd needed
some sleep. So she'd given her body and hair a decent
scrub before falling into that outrageously comfortable bed naked, since she hadn't been able to bear
putting on her filthy clothes again—not when she
was so clean.

Her sleep had been fitful, due to the comfortable-
ness of the bed—she was used to sleeping on hard
surfaces covered with nothing but pieces of card-
board or, if she was lucky and had managed to get a
night in a shelter, a hard mattress covered by a thin
blanket—and she'd kept waking up. Her sleep was
always light, in case of threats, but even so she'd felt
okay when she'd woken this morning.

There had been a set of clothes left outside her
door, which she'd snatched up and put on, glorying in
the feel of soft, clean cotton against her skin. Coffee
and a fresh warm croissant had been left along with
the clothes, and she'd devoured both in seconds. She
had still been hungry, but then Camille had come, a
little less scornful than she'd been the night before,
and given her an introduction to her duties.

There'd been no time for more food.

She was supposed to have spent no more than
half an hour in the library—concentrating on dusting the shelves, since the duke was most particular
about them—before moving on to the formal sitting

room next door. But she had a horrible suspicion that she'd been in here longer than half an hour. And she hadn't even touched the shelves yet.

She'd just got very interested in some of the books, and hadn't been able to resist taking one off the shelf and opening it up.

Back when she'd been smaller, when her mother had still been around, she'd used to love going to the library and reading, and books were something she'd missed on the streets. And back further still, when she'd been very young, her father had read to her—

But, no, she wasn't going to think of her father.

She needed to be more alert to her surroundings, that was what she needed to be, because this wretched duke was always sneaking up on her.

Quickly, she closed the book and put it back. 'I wasn't reading,' she said, picking up her cloth and polish. 'I was just polishing the shelf.' She ran the cloth over the already gleaming wood a couple of times. 'It's very dirty.'

'Which book was it?'

Again that voice—a deep, dark purr that felt like soft velvet brushing against her skin. It made her shiver and she didn't like it…not one bit.

Clutching her cleaning equipment, Leonie got to her feet and turned around, only to have the words she'd been going to say die in her throat.

The duke was leaning one powerful shoulder casually against the doorframe, his hands in his pockets. He was in perfectly tailored black suit trousers today, and a pristine white shirt with the sleeves rolled up to his elbows, revealing strong wrists and sleekly muscled forearms. It was plain, simple clothing that set off his sheer physical beauty to perfection, accentuating the aristocratic lines of his face, the straight black brows, the sharply carved mouth and the deep emerald glitter of his eyes.

He seemed different from the man he'd been the night before. There was an energy about him that hadn't been present the previous evening. It was oddly compelling and that made her wary.

Everything about this man made her wary.

He raised a brow in that imperious way he had. 'You were going to say something?'

Leonie was irritated to feel a blush rising in her cheeks, because she had a feeling he'd noticed her reaction to him and was amused by it.

'No,' she said, wishing she had her knife on her. Because although he hadn't made a move towards her, she felt the threat he presented all the same. 'Is there anything you need…uh…*monsieur*?' She couldn't quite bring herself to say *Your Grace*.

A smile curled his mouth, though it didn't look like an amused smile. More as if he was…satisfied.

'Not at all. Just coming to see how my newest staff member is settling in. Is everything to your liking?'

'Yes, thank you.' She kept a tight grip on her cloth and polish. 'Camille said she would find me another room to sleep—'

'I think not,' he interrupted, with the casual arrogance of a man who was used to his word being law. 'You'll stay in the room you're in.'

Leonie wasn't unhappy with that—especially when she hadn't had a chance to use that amazing bath yet, and also didn't like being in close proximity to a lot of people—but she didn't like his automatic assumption that she could be told what to do.

And your need to fight is what gets you into trouble.

This was very true. And there was also another problem. A problem she'd foreseen the night before and yet had dismissed.

In accepting a bed for the night, and now a job, she'd had a tiny taste of what her life might be like off the streets.

Having a shower whenever she wanted it…having clean sheets and clean clothes. Having food brought to her and having something to do that wasn't figuring out how to shoplift her next meal or begging for coins. Being safe behind walls and locked doors.

Just a tiny taste. Enough to know she didn't want to give it up—not just yet.

This is how they suck you in. You should have run…

She swallowed, clutching her cleaning implements even tighter. It was too late to run now—too late to decide that life on the streets was better than being in this house and working for this duke. Like Persephone from the myth, she'd had a bite of the pomegranate and now she was trapped in the Underworld.

Which makes him Hades.

And a very fine Hades he made, too. No wonder she found him dangerous. He was the snake in the garden, offering temptation...

'I don't need a special room,' she said, because her need to fight was so ingrained she couldn't stop herself. 'I'm happy to sleep wherever the other employees—'

'As I said, you will stay in the room you've been given.'

'Why?'

'Because I said so,' he replied easily. 'I'm the duke and what I say goes.' That smile was still playing around his fascinating mouth. 'Which reminds me—I usually have a formal job interview with my employees, and since you didn't have one, I suggest we schedule one for tonight. Over dinner.'

Instantly all her alarm bells went off at once. A job interview over dinner? That didn't sound right at all. Not that she had any experience with job interviews, but still...

She gave him a suspicious look. 'Job interviews are usually in offices during the day, not over dinner.'

'Astute, *gatita*. If being in an office would make you more comfortable, I can have dinner served to us there.'

Leonie scowled. 'I'm not sleeping with you.'

He raised both brows this time. 'Have I asked you to sleep with me?'

'No, but when a man asks a woman to dinner he expects certain things. Men always do.'

'You appear to have a very poor opinion of men—though I suppose that's understandable. We're not especially good examples of the human race.' His eyes glittered strangely. 'It's also true that I'm a particularly bad example. But I don't have any sexual designs on you, if that's what you're worried about.'

She *had* been worried about it. The threat of sexual violence was ever-present for a woman on her own on the streets. So why did him telling her that he had no sexual designs on her make her feel almost…disappointed?

'That's all very well,' she said, ignoring the feeling, 'but I don't trust you.'

He shifted, drawing her attention to his powerful body, making her aware of him in a disturbingly physical way.

'Fair enough. We've only just met after all. Bring your knife with you. And if I try anything romantic feel free to cut me with it.'

'Or you could just decide we don't need to have an interview,' she suggested. 'After all, you've already employed me.'

'It's true—I have. But the process is the process. I can't just let anyone into my house. Security checks need to be done…reference checks, et cetera. It's all very tiresome but absolutely necessary.' He paused, his gaze sharpening on her. 'Especially when said employee hasn't even given me her name.'

Leonie took a silent breath. She should have given it to him last night when he'd asked. What did it matter if he knew? She'd only wanted to retain a little bit of autonomy, but now she'd turned it into a big deal and maybe he thought she was trying to hide something, or that she was on the run from something.

Not the actual truth, which was that she was only a girl who'd been discarded by both parents. A girl nobody wanted.

Her gut tightened. He certainly didn't need to know that. And, anyway, her name was her own and it was hers to give. No one had the right to know it.

Why don't you give him a fake one, then?

She could. But that would be giving in, regardless of whether it was a fake name or not, and something inside her wouldn't let her do that.

What was it about him that had her wanting to fight him all the time? She'd never had such strong reactions to a man before. Admittedly, she hadn't come into contact with a lot of men, since it was better safety-wise to avoid them, but the few she'd had run-ins with hadn't endeared themselves to her. But this man...

He made her want to fight, to stand her ground, kick back. He also made her feel physical things she hadn't felt before in her entire life. A kind of shivery ache. A prickly restlessness. The stupid desire to poke at him just to see what he'd do. What on earth was that?

You know what it is.

But Leonie didn't want to think about it. She couldn't afford to—not when she was seconds away from catastrophe. Who knew how long this job would last? Or when she'd be turned out back on to the streets again?

She'd got herself into this situation, and if she was very lucky it would mean good things for her. So the most logical thing to do now was to be careful with the dangerous panther that lounged on the branch above her head. To keep her head down and perhaps not present herself as so much prey. Keep a low profile and not struggle. If she did that well he might even forget she existed and leave her alone.

So she said nothing, dragging her gaze away from him and looking at the ground instead.

'Ah, so that's how it's to be, hmm?'

Again, he sounded just like that panther—all low and purring and sleek.

'Come to my study when you finish up today. I'll tell Camille that you're expected.'

She nodded silently, and when she finally looked up the doorway was empty.

He'd gone.

CHAPTER FOUR

CRISTIANO FROWNED AT the clock on the mantelpiece, an unexpected impatience gathering inside him. Leonie was late and he suspected it was intentional, since Camille wouldn't have kept her working if she was expected to attend a meeting with him.

And she was definitely expected to attend.

He supposed he could have had the conversation with her in the library earlier that day, rather than make a performance of it over dinner. But trust was a difficult thing. You couldn't compel it and you couldn't buy it—it could only be given.

Which made him a liar in some respects, because he was absolutely planning a seduction. Except sex wasn't the goal. He was planning on seducing her curious mind instead.

He found himself energised by the prospect. It had been a long time since he'd had to exert himself for a woman—for anyone, for that matter—and the idea was more exciting than he'd anticipated. Lately his life of unmitigated pleasure had begun to pall, and it made a nice change to have to put his brain to good use instead of his body.

The thought of de Riero's shock as his daughter was revealed was…

The feeling of satisfaction was vicious, hot, and he had to force it back down—hard. He couldn't let emotion rule him. Not given the mistake he'd made the last time he'd tried to confront de Riero, blundering around in a blind rage, sending his son straight back into the other man's arms.

This time he needed to be casual, detached. Keep his revenge cold.

Mastering himself once more, Cristiano checked the time again, allowing himself some amusement at his own impatience, then crossed over to his desk. Since she was late, he might as well do something. It wouldn't do for her to find him cooling his heels and watching the clock for her arrival; he wasn't a man who waited for anyone, still less looked as if he was.

There were a few business matters he had to attend to, a few calls to make, and he made them, keeping an ear out for the door. And sure enough, ten minutes later, while he was in the middle of a conversation with a business acquaintance, he heard a soft knock.

'Enter,' he said, then turned his chair around so his back was to the room, continuing with his call.

It was petty, but he'd never been above a little pettiness. It would do her good to wait for him—especially since he'd spent the last ten minutes waiting for her.

He carried on with his call in a leisurely fashion, in no hurry to end it since his acquaintance was amusing, and only when the other man had to go did he end the call and turn his chair back around.

Leonie was standing near one of the ornate wooden shelves he kept stocked with his favourite reading material—business texts, philosophy, sociology and a few novels thrown in the mix—staring fixedly at the spines. She held herself very tense, her shoulders and spine stiff, that waterfall of beautiful hair lying sleek and silky down her back.

He had the sense that she wasn't actually looking at the books at all. She was waiting for him. Good.

'Good evening, *gatita*,' he said lazily, leaning back in his chair. 'You're late.'

Slowly, she turned to him, and his gaze was instantly drawn to the dark circles beneath her eyes. Her pretty face looked pale, her big violet-blue eyes shadowed. One hand was in the pocket of her black trousers—clutching that knife, no doubt.

A feeling he wasn't expecting tightened in his chest. He ignored it, raising a brow at her. 'Well? Any particular reason you're late to your job interview?'

Her determined little chin lifted. 'Because you distracted me in the library I didn't get my work done on time, so I had to make it up at the end of the day.'

He almost laughed. She did like testing him,

didn't she? 'I see. Nothing whatsoever to do with the fact that I caught you reading, hmm?'

Colour bloomed across her delicate cheekbones. 'No.'

Which was an outright lie and they both knew it.

Highly amused, he grinned. 'And you took some time to go back to your room for you knife, also, I think?'

Her forearm flexed above where her hand disappeared into her pocket, as if she was squeezing her fingers around the handle of something. But this time she didn't deny it.

'You said I could bring it.'

'It's true. I did.'

He got up from the chair and came around the side of his desk, noting the way she tensed at his approach. She was very wary of him. As wary as she'd been the night before. Understandable, of course, and it was an obvious sign of distrust. In fact, he could probably gauge her progression in trusting him through the way she acted around him physically.

It made him wonder, though, exactly what had happened to her out there on the Parisian streets. How she'd managed to survive. What had happened to Hélène? Why hadn't she gone to her father and told him she was still alive...?

So many questions.

If he wanted answers, he had some work to do.

He moved over to the fireplace against one wall,

opposite the bookshelves. He'd had one of his staff light a fire even though it wasn't particularly cold, mainly because it made the room feel more welcoming. The fire crackled pleasantly, casting its orange glow over Leonie's beautiful hair.

She watched him as if he was a dangerous animal she had to be cautious about, yet her gaze kept flicking to the fire as if she wanted to get close to it. As if she was cold.

'You're afraid of me,' he said, and didn't make it a question. 'I can assure you that you have no need to be.'

Her gaze flickered. 'I'm not afraid.'

But the response sounded as if it had been made by rote—as if that was always her answer, whether it was true or not. It made sense, though. When you were small and female you were viewed as prey by certain people, which meant fear wasn't something you could afford. Fear was weakness. Especially when there was no one to protect you.

Had she ever had anyone to protect her? Or had she had to do it herself?

That tight feeling in his chest shifted again. It had been such a long time since he'd felt anything remotely resembling pity or sympathy that he wasn't sure what it was at first. But then he knew. He didn't like the idea of her being on her own. He didn't like the idea of her not being protected. How strange.

'Then come closer.' He thrust his hands in his

pockets so he looked less intimidating. 'You want to be near the fire. Don't think I hadn't noticed.'

She didn't like that—he could see the tension ripple through her. Perhaps he was wrong to test her. But if he wanted her trust he had to start somewhere, and having her be less wary around him physically was certainly one way of doing it.

He remained still, not moving, keeping his hands in his pockets, silently daring her. She was brave, not to mention stubborn, and he suspected that if he kept challenging her she'd rise to it.

Sure enough, after a couple of tense moments, she gave a shrug, as if it didn't matter, and then came slowly across the room to stand on the opposite side of the fireplace. Her expression was carefully blank, and when she got closer to the flames she held out her hands to warm them.

Ostensibly she looked as if nothing bothered her and she was perfectly comfortable. But she wasn't. He could feel the tension vibrating in the air around her.

She was like a wild animal, ready to start at the slightest sound or motion.

'There,' he murmured. 'That's not so bad, is it?'

She flicked him an impatient look. 'I'm not afraid of you. I have a knife.'

'Good. Keep that knife about your person at all times.' He turned slightly, noting how she tensed at his movement. 'So, nameless *gatita*. I suppose my first question to you is why on earth were you spray-painting my limo at two in the morning?'

Her attention was on the flames, but he suspected she was still very aware of him. 'Why shouldn't I be spray-painting your limo at two in the morning?'

'That's not the correct answer,' he reproved mildly. 'Don't you think I'm owed an explanation, considering it was my property you vandalised?'

Irritation crossed her features. 'Fine. The people I was with dared me to. So I did.'

'And if they dared you to jump off the Eiffel Tower you'd do the same?'

'Probably.' She gave him a sidelong glance. 'You can't back down—not even once. Not if you don't want to be a target.'

Ah, so now they were getting to it. 'I see. And these people are your friends?'

He thought not. Not considering how a one-hundred-euro note had been enough to pay for her name.

She shook her head. 'Just some people I was hanging around with.'

'At two in the morning? Didn't you have somewhere else to go?'

Her lashes fell, limned in gold by the firelight. 'It's…safer to be around other people sometimes.'

The tight thing coiled in his chest shifted around yet again, because even though she hadn't said it outright he knew. No, she didn't have anywhere to go, and she didn't want to admit it.

Proud *gatita*.

'I'm not sure those people were very safe,' he murmured. 'Considering how your night ended.'

She gave a shrug. 'Could have been worse.'

'Indeed. You could have spent another night on the streets.'

There was no response to that, though he didn't expect her either to confirm or deny it—not given how reluctant she was to give him any information about herself. Clearly telling her that he knew who she was wouldn't go down well, so he definitely wasn't going to reveal that in a hurry.

A small silence fell, broken only by the crackling of the fire.

'Will you sit down?' he asked after a moment. 'The chair behind you will allow you to stay close to the fire if you're cold.'

She gave him another sidelong glance, then made a show of looking around the room, as if trying to locate the chair. Then, without any hurry, she moved over to it and sat down, leaning back, ostensibly relaxed, though she'd put her hand in her pocket again, holding on to her knife.

There was another armchair opposite hers, so he sat down in that one. A low coffee table was positioned between them, which should present her with a safety barrier if she needed it.

'So what now?' she asked, staring at him, her chin set at a stubborn angle.

'Tell me a little about yourself. If not your name,

then at least a few things that will give me an idea about the kind of person I've just employed.'

'Why do you want to know that?'

He smiled. 'This isn't supposed to be a debate—merely a request for information.'

'Why do you need information?'

Persistent, wasn't she? Not to mention challenging. Good. His life had been without any challenges lately, and he could use the excitement.

'Well, since you won't give me your name, I need some indication of whether you're likely to make off with all the silverware.' He paused, considering whether or not to let her know just how much leeway he was allowing her. Why not? If she was testing him, he could test her. 'I do a background check on all employees who are granted access to my house, in other words. For safety reasons, you understand?'

A little crease appeared between her red-gold brows. 'How can you be unsafe? Here?'

Of course she'd find that surprising. Especially if she was living on the streets. She no doubt thought nothing could harm him here, and to a certain extent she was right. Physically, he was safe. But four walls and bodyguards—even if he employed any—didn't equal safety. You could have all the physical protection in the world and still end up broken and bleeding.

Luckily for him, his wounds had healed. And no one could see the scars but him.

'You can be unsafe anywhere,' he said dryly. 'In my experience you can never be too careful.'

'And what is your experience?'

He almost answered her. Almost. Sneaky kitten.

Cristiano smiled. 'It's supposed to be your job interview, *gatita*, not mine. I already have a job.'

'And so do I. You gave it to me, remember?'

'I do. Which means I can take it back whenever I like.'

She sniffed, glancing over to the fire once more. 'I might be more inclined to answer your questions if you answered some of mine.'

Well, this was an interesting tactic...

'That's not how a job interview works,' he said, amused by how she kept on pushing. 'Also, if you'll remember, I gave you my name last night.'

An irritated expression flitted across her face. She shifted in her seat and he didn't miss how her hand had fallen away from the pocket where her knife was kept.

So. Progress.

'I don't know why you keep asking.' Her sweet, husky voice had an edge to it. 'Not when you could just threaten me and be done with it.'

'Threats are effective, it's true. But ultimately they're not very exciting.' He watched her face. 'Not when it's much more fun to convince you to give it to me willingly.'

She flushed. 'You're very sure of yourself.'

'Of course I'm sure of myself. I'm a duke.'

'Duke of what?'

Good question. And because he was enjoying himself, and because it had been a long time since any woman had provided him with this much amusement, he answered it.

'Weren't you listening last night? I'm the Fifteenth Duke of San Lorenzo. It's a small duchy in Andalusia.'

She gave him a measuring look. 'What are you doing in Paris?'

'Business.' He smiled. 'Catching vandals spray-painting rude words on my limo.'

She gave another little sniff at that, but the colour in her cheeks deepened—which was a good thing considering how pale she'd been.

'You didn't sleep well, *gatita*,' he observed quietly. 'But I did tell Camille to let you sleep in a little this morning.'

She blinked and looked away, shifting around in her seat. 'The bed was…uncomfortable. And I'd had a long shower—too long.'

Well, he knew for a fact that the bed wasn't uncomfortable, since he had the same one in his room here. And as for the shower…that may have been the case. But he suspected she hadn't slept well because she wasn't used to having a bed at all.

'What do you care anyway?' she added irritably.

'I care because I like my employees to do a good job. And they can't if they're not well rested.'

'Or well fed,' she muttered.

He thought she probably hadn't meant him to hear

that, but unfortunately for her he had excellent hearing. So she was hungry, was she? Again, understandable. If she lived on the streets, decent food must be hard to come by.

How lucky, then, that he'd organised a very good dinner.

Right on cue, there was a knock at the door.

She sat up, tension gathering around her again, instantly on the alert.

'Enter,' he said, watching her response as several staff members came in, bearing trays of the food he'd ordered.

Her eyes went wide as he directed them to put the food on the coffee table between them, including cutlery and plates, not to mention a couple of glasses and a bottle of extremely good red wine from his cellar.

'I told you there would be dinner,' he murmured as his staff arranged the food and then quietly withdrew.

Leonie had sat forward, her gaze fixed on the food on the table. It was a simple meal—a fresh garden salad and excellent steak, along with some warm, crusty bread and salted butter. All her earlier wariness had dissipated, to be replaced by a different kind of tension.

Her hands were clasped tightly in her lap.

She was hungry.

He became aware that her cheeks were slightly hollow, and her figure, now it wasn't swamped by that giant hoodie, was very slender. Probably too slender.

No, she wasn't just hungry—she was starving.

That tightness in his chest grew sharp edges, touching on that dangerous volcanic anger of his. Anger at how this lovely, spirited woman had ended up where she had. On the streets. Left to fend for herself with only a knife.

Left to starve.

Hélène had taken her and disappeared, letting Victor de Riero think she and his daughter were dead, but what had led her to do that? Had de Riero treated them badly? Was there something that had stopped Leonie from seeking him out?

A memory trickled through his consciousness…a small green-eyed boy running into de Riero's arms in fear…

Fear of you.

Red tinged the edges of Cristiano's vision and it took a massive effort to shove the rage back down where it had come from, to ignore the memory in his head. He had to do it. There would be no mistakes, not this time.

But her challenging him so continually was dangerous for them both. It roused his long-dormant emotions and that couldn't happen. Which meant she had to give him the answers he needed. Tonight. Now.

As she reached out towards the food Cristiano shot out a hand and closed his fingers around her narrow wrist. 'Oh, no, *gatita*. I've given you enough leeway. If you want to eat, you must pay me with some answers first.'

Leonie froze, her heart thudding hard in her ears, panic flooding through her. When his fingers had tightened her free hand had gone instantly to her knife, to pull it out and slash him with it.

'No,' he said, very calmly and with so much authority that for some strange reason her panic eased.

Because although his grip was firm, he wasn't pulling at her. He was only holding her. His fingers burned against her skin like a manacle of fire—except that wasn't painful, either. Or rather, it wasn't pain that she felt but a kind of prickling heat that swept up her arm and over the rest of her body.

She felt hypnotised by the sight of his fingers around her wrist. Long, strong and tanned. Competent hands. Not cruel hands.

'You'd stop me eating just to get what you want?' she asked hoarsely, not looking at him, staring instead at that warm, long-fingered hand gripping her wrist.

'No,' he repeated, in that deep, authoritarian voice. 'But I've given you food and a bed. A job that you'll be paid for. I haven't touched you except for twice—once when I grabbed you last night, and once now. I've given you my name and told you a few things about me. I have let you into my home.'

He paused, as if he wanted those words to sink in. And, as much as she didn't want them to, they did.

'I'm not asking for your date of birth or your passport number, or the number of your bank account. I'm not even asking for your surname. All I want is your first name. It's a small thing in return for all that, don't you think? After all, it was you who decided to deface my car, not me.'

Then, much to her shock, he let her go.

Her heart was beating very fast and she could still feel the imprint of his fingertips on her skin. It was as if he'd scorched her, and it made thinking very difficult.

But he was right about one thing. He wasn't asking for much. And he hadn't hurt her or been cruel. He *had* given her a bed and a job, and now there was food. And he hadn't withheld his name from her the way she had withheld hers from him.

She didn't trust him, but giving him this one small thing wouldn't hurt. After all, there were probably plenty of Leonies around. He couldn't know that she was Leonie de Riero, the forgotten daughter of Victor de Riero, the rich Spanish magnate, who'd tossed her and her mother out because he'd wanted a son. Or at least that was what her mother had told her.

'Leonie,' she said quietly, still staring at her wrist, part of her amazed she didn't have scorch marks there from his hand. 'My name is Leonie.'

There was a silence.

She glanced up and found his green gaze on hers,

deep and dark as forests and full of dangerous wild things. She couldn't look away.

There was a kind of humming in the air around them, and the prickling heat that had swept over her skin was spreading out. Warming her entire body. Making her feel restless and hot and hungry. But not for food.

'Thank you,' the duke said gravely.

He was not triumphant or smug, nor even showing that lazy amusement she'd come to associate with him. It was as if her name had been an important gift and he was receiving it with all the solemnity that entailed.

'Pleased to met you, Leonie.'

Just for a moment she thought he might reach out and take her hand, shake it. And, strangely, she almost wanted him to, so she could feel his fingers on her skin again. How odd to want to touch someone after so long actively avoiding it.

But he didn't take her hand. Instead he gestured to the food.

'Eat.' His mouth curled. 'Not that I was going to stop you from eating.'

Leonie decided not to say anything to that. She was too hungry anyway.

Not wanting to draw his attention, she didn't load her plate with too much food and she tried to eat slowly. It was all unbelievably delicious, but she wanted to pace herself. It had been a while since she'd eaten rich food and she didn't want to make herself sick. But it tasted so good—especially the fresh vegetables.

The duke poured her a glass of wine and she had a sip—and her toes just about curled in the plain black leather shoes she'd been given. Everything tasted amazing. She wanted to eat and drink all of it.

He didn't eat—merely sat there toying with a glass of wine in a leisurely fashion and studying her. It was disconcerting.

'You're not hungry?' she asked, feeling self-conscious.

Had she been gorging herself? She didn't want to give away how starving she was, wary of him asking more questions that she wasn't prepared to answer.

What does it matter if he knows you're homeless?

Perhaps it didn't matter. Perhaps it was only instinct that prevented her from revealing more, the long years of being wary and mistrustful settling into a reflex she couldn't ignore. Then again, there were reasons for her mistrust and wariness. She'd seen many young women in the same situation as herself fall victim to unscrupulous men because they'd trusted the wrong person, revealed the wrong thing.

Easier to keep to oneself, not let anyone close and stay alive.

It was a habit her wary, bitter mother had instilled in her long before she was on the streets anyway, and she'd seen no reason to change it.

Then again, although trusting this particular man might be a bridge too far, it was clear he wasn't here to hurt her. He'd had ample opportunity to do so and hadn't, so either he was saving it for a specific time or he wasn't going to do anything to her at all.

Maybe she could relax a little. Perhaps part of her reluctance to tell him anything had more to do with what he'd think of her, a dirty Parisian street kid, than whether he'd harm her. Not that she cared what he thought of her. At all.

'No, not hungry right now.' He leaned back in his chair, his wine glass held between long fingers. 'Did Camille not feed you enough?'

Despite all her justifications, she could feel her cheeks get hot. When she'd been turned out of the dilapidated apartment she'd shared with her mother, after her mother hadn't ever returned home, she'd had to fend for herself. And that hadn't allowed for such luxuries as pride. So why she was blushing now because he'd spotted her hunger, she had no idea.

'Just hungry today,' she muttered, not willing to give him anything else just yet. Mainly because she'd been doing nothing but resist for so long she couldn't remember how to surrender.

'I think not.' His tone was casual. 'I think you're starving.'

She tensed. Had the way she'd been eating given her away? 'I'm not——'

'Your cheeks are hollow and you're far too thin.' His gaze was very sharp, though his posture was relaxed. 'You're homeless, aren't you?'

Did you really think you could keep it from him?

Damn. Why did he have to be so observant? Why couldn't be like all the other rich people in the world who never saw the people living on the streets? Who were blind to them? Why couldn't he have simply called the police when he'd grabbed her the night before and got her carted away to the cells?

Why do you even care?

She had no answer to that except to wish it wasn't true. Sadly, though, it was true. She did care. She didn't want him to know that she was homeless—that she had no one and nothing. And she especially didn't want him to know that she'd once been the daughter of a very rich man who'd left her to rot on the streets like so much unwanted trash. Her mother had been very clear on that point.

Except, all the wanting in the world wasn't going to change the fact that he'd picked up on a few things she'd hoped he wouldn't see and had drawn his own conclusions. Correct conclusions. So was there any point in denying it now? She could pretend she had a home and a family, but he'd see through that pretty quickly. He was that kind of man.

So, since pretending was out, Leonie decided on belligerence instead. She stared back at him, daring him to pass judgement on her. 'And if I am?'

His gaze roamed over her face, irritatingly making the heat in her cheeks deepen even more. 'And nothing,' he said at last. 'It was merely an observation.'

'Don't you want to know where and why and how

it happened? Whether I'm a drug addict or an alcoholic? Why haven't I found somewhere to go or a shelter to stay in?'

'Not particularly.' His green eyes gleamed. 'But if you want to tell me any of those things I'm happy to listen.'

That surprised her. She'd been expecting him to push for more information since he'd been so emphatic about her name before. Yet apparently not.

A strange feeling settled in her gut. Almost as if she'd wanted him to ask so she could tell him and was disappointed that he hadn't.

To cover her surprise, she reached for another piece of bread, spreading it liberally with the delicious butter and eating it in slow, careful bites.

'I'll have Camille make sure you get enough to eat,' he said after a moment. 'I won't have you going hungry here.'

She swallowed the last bit of bread. 'Don't tell her—'

'I won't. Your secret's safe with me.'

She didn't want it to be reassuring, yet it was. Not that she cared about what Camille thought, but still… Questions would be asked and she didn't want questions. She didn't want to have to explain her situation to anyone—including this powerful, yet oddly reassuring duke.

He could protect you.

The thought was a discomforting one. She'd protected herself well enough for nearly six years, so why would she need him?

You need someone, though.

No, she didn't.

She picked up her wine and took another sip, allowing the rich, dark flavour to settle on her tongue. It made her a little dizzy, but she didn't mind that.

He began to ask her a few more questions, though these were solely about how she'd found the work today and whether she had what she needed to do her job, so she answered them. Then they had a discussion about what other tasks she might like to tackle and how she'd prefer to be paid—cash, since she didn't have a bank account.

The conversation wasn't personal, his questions were not intrusive, and he didn't make any more of those unexpected movements. And after maybe another half an hour had passed his phone went. Since it was apparently urgent, he excused himself to answer it.

Leonie settled back in the chair and finished her wine. It was very warm in the room, and she was very full, and since they were both sensations she had almost never felt she wanted to enjoy them for a little while.

The deep, rich sound of his voice as he talked to whoever he was talking to was lulling her. There was warmth and texture to that voice, and it was comforting in a way she couldn't describe.

Maybe it was that voice. Or maybe it was the wine

and food. Maybe it was fire crackling pleasantly in the fireplace. Or maybe it was simply the fact that she'd barely slept a wink the night before, but she found her eyes beginning to close.

It took a lot of effort to keep them open.

Too much effort.

She closed them, all her muscles relaxing, along with her ever-present vigilance.

And then she fell asleep.

At some point she became aware that she was in someone's arms and was being carried somewhere. Normally that would have been enough to have her struggling wildly and waking up. But a familiar warm and spicy scent wound around her, and a comforting heat against her side was easing her instinctive panic.

And instead of struggling she relaxed. Letting the heat and that familiar scent soothe her. Feeling those arms tighten around her.

Where she was being carried, she didn't know, and a minute or so later she didn't care.

She was already asleep again.

CHAPTER FIVE

CRISTIANO MADE AN effort over the next week to keep an eye on Leonie in an unobtrusive way, stopping by wherever she was working to exchange a few words with her. Sometimes it was just that—a few words—and sometimes it was more of a conversation.

And slowly she began to relax around him. She no longer tensed when he appeared, and during the last two visits, she hadn't even scowled.

He counted it a victory.

Of course the real victory had been that night in his study, when she'd finally given him her name.

Reaching out to grab her wrist had been a gamble, but she'd had to learn that he meant business and that he had his limits. He wasn't a man to be toyed with. Besides, he hadn't been asking for much—just her name.

She'd seemed to understand and the gamble had paid off. She hadn't given him anything else, but he hadn't pushed. He knew when to insist and when to back off. She'd eventually give him what he wanted—he was sure of it.

He'd been even more sure when he'd finished his phone call and turned around to find that she'd fallen asleep in her chair. He hadn't wanted to wake her, since the shadows under her eyes had been pronounced, but nor had he wanted to leave her sleeping in an uncomfortable position. So, compelled by an instinct he hadn't felt in years, he'd gathered her into his arms and carried her up to her room.

Another gamble, considering how hyper-vigilant she was. But she hadn't woken. Or at least she hadn't panicked. Her lovely red-gold eyelashes had fluttered and her muscles had tensed, and then, just as quickly, she'd relaxed against him. As if she'd decided she was safe.

A mistake on her part, because he wasn't safe—not in any way—but he'd liked the way she'd felt in his arms. Liked the way she'd relaxed against him as if she didn't need to fear him. Liked it too much, truth be told.

Anna had never nestled sleepily in his arms. She'd never been comfortable with his displays of affection. But he was a deeply physical man and that was how he expressed it. She had also known his darkest secret, known the damage he was capable of, and although she'd never said it outright he knew she'd always judged him for it.

He'd tried to contain himself for her, change himself for her, but it hadn't been enough in the end. Victor de Riero had offered her what Cristiano hadn't been able to, and so she'd left him.

But it was dangerous to think of Anna, so he'd shoved his memories of her away and ignored the way Leonie had felt in his arms.

Leonie hadn't mentioned it the next day when he'd stopped by the room where she was dusting, so he hadn't mentioned it, either, merely giving her a greeting and then going on his way.

Which was what he'd done the next couple of days, too, only stopping for longer on the subsequent days after that. And the day before, not only had he not had a scowl, but he thought he might have had a smile. Or at least the beginnings of one.

It was very definitely a start.

But he needed to do more.

He wasn't normally an impatient man, since he never wanted anything enough to get impatient about it, but the thought of revenge had definitely put him in an impatient mood. He needed to gain her trust and then either get her to tell him who she was or reveal that he already knew in a way that wouldn't frighten her off.

After that, he had to ascertain her feelings about her father and find out whether she'd agree to let him widen her job description, as it were. In return for a sizeable bonus, naturally.

It was a good plan, and one he was sure would work, but it would require a certain delicacy. So far he'd done well, but more needed to be accomplished— and faster.

It was a pity trust wasn't one of those things that could be compelled.

He was reflecting on that as he arrived back home late one night the following week. He'd come from a party that had started out as tedious, only to descend into unpleasant when he'd heard Victor de Riero's name being bandied about in a business discussion.

Normally that wouldn't have caused him any concern. He'd detached himself so completely from what had happened fifteen years ago that he could even have attended the same party as the man and not felt a thing.

Yet tonight even the sound of that name had set his anger burning so fiercely that some disconnected part of him had been amazed at the intensity of his emotions when for so long he'd felt nothing. It had been disturbing, and it had made him even more certain that he must move his revenge plan on faster— because the quicker he dealt with it, the easier it would be to put out the fire of his anger once and for all.

He'd left the party early, full of that intense directionless anger, and was still in a foul temper now, as he arrived home. He'd been intending to sit in the library alone, with a very good Scotch, so his mood was not improved when he found that the library was already occupied by Leonie, kneeling on the floor in front of the bookshelves once again.

She was still in her uniform, and there were cleaning implements next to her, even though it was nearly midnight and she should be in bed, asleep. Something jolted in his chest at the sight of that familiar red-gold skein hanging down on her back.

He remembered carrying her to bed that night— how that hair had brushed against his forearm and then drifted over the backs of his hands as he'd bent over to lay her down on the mattress. It had felt very silky, and the urge to touch it, to sift his fingers through it, had gripped him once again. She'd felt light in his arms, but very soft and warm and feminine, and she'd smelled subtly of the rose-scented soap her bathroom had been stocked with.

He'd been very good at not paying attention to his physical reactions around her. Very good at not thinking about that moment of chemistry in his study that night when he'd put his fingers around her wrist, touched her soft skin. And it had been soft, her pulse frantic beneath his fingertips.

It hadn't been a problem before. He was always in complete control of himself, even when it looked to the rest of the world as if he wasn't. Yet right now, looking at her kneeling there, that control seemed suddenly very tenuous.

There'd been enough beautiful women at the party tonight for him to take his pick if it was sex he wanted. He didn't have to have her. She'd be a virgin, too—he'd bet his dukedom on it—and he wasn't into virgins. They were complicated, and the last thing he needed was more complications.

Yet that didn't put a stop to the hunger that

gripped him, and his temper, already on a knife-edge, worsened.

Meirda, what was she doing here? Hadn't she finished her work? There were plenty of chairs around. Why wasn't she sitting on one of them? But, most importantly, why wasn't she safely in bed and out of his reach? And why did he always find her poring over a book?

He prowled up behind her, where she knelt, but she didn't look around, once again absorbed in whatever she was reading.

'You can take that upstairs if you want,' he said, unable to keep the growl out of his voice. 'You don't have to sit on the floor.'

She gave a little start, then sprang to her feet, turning around quickly. Her violet-blue eyes were very wide, and one hand automatically went to her pocket—as if her knife was still there and not where he'd seen it last, on her bedside table.

And then, as she took in his presence, her posture relaxed as quickly as it had tensed. 'Oh…' she breathed. 'It's you.'

He should have been pleased by how quickly she'd calmed, since it indicated more progress towards her trusting him. But tonight he wasn't pleased. Tonight it rubbed against his vile temper like salt in a wound. She was the daughter of his enemy and he was going to use her to get his revenge on that *hijo de puta*. She should be afraid of him. He was dangerous—and most especially when he was angry.

Hadn't Anna always told him that he frightened her? She'd been right to be scared. He was capable of such destruction when he let his emotions get the better of him. This little kitten should be cowering, not relaxing as if she was safe.

'Yes, it is,' he agreed, his temper burning with a sullen heat. 'What are you doing in the library at this time of night?' It came out as an accusation, which wasn't helpful, but he didn't bother to adjust his tone. He wasn't in the mood for adjusting himself for anyone tonight. 'You should go to bed.'

'I was working late.' Her forehead creased, her violet-blue gaze studying him. 'Are you all right?'

A dart of something sharp he couldn't identify shot through him. Was his temper that noticeable? Maybe it was. He hadn't exactly been hiding it after all. Still, he hadn't been asked that question in a very long time. Years, possibly. Not by his staff, not his few close friends, not his lovers. And the fact that this homeless girl should be the first one to have even a fleeting concern for his wellbeing annoyed him all the more.

He smiled without humour. 'Of course. Why would you imagine I'm anything other than all right?'

'Because you're...' She made a gesture at him.

'Because I'm what?' He took a leisurely step towards her. 'Have you been watching me, *gatita*?'

Her cheeks flooded with telltale colour. 'No, I haven't.'

A lie. She *had* been watching him. How interesting.

You should order her upstairs. Away from you. Nothing good comes from your temper—you know this already.

Oh, he knew. He knew all too well. But he was tired of having to do what he always did, which was to shove that temper away. Beat it down so no one would ever know it was there. Tired of having to pretend he didn't feel it, of having to restrain himself all the time.

Dios, she was the one who'd brought all this to the surface again. This was her fault if it was anyone's.

So what are you going to do? Punish her?

He ignored the thought, taking another step towards her. 'I think you have. I think you've been watching me. And why is that?' He let his voice drop to a low purr. 'Do you see something you like?'

Something flickered through her eyes, though he couldn't tell what it was. It wasn't fear, though, and he didn't understand. She was normally wary, and yet she wasn't wary now, which was strange. Had he done his job already? Did she trust him?

Silly *gatita*. Perhaps he should show her what she had to be afraid about.

He closed the distance between them, crowding her very purposefully back against the bookshelves, and this time obvious alarm rippled across her pretty face. He was standing close enough to feel the warmth of her body and inhale the faint, sweet scent of roses. Close enough to see the pulse beating fast beneath the pale skin at the base of her throat.

Fool. Giving in to your temper will undo all the progress you've made, and you swore you wouldn't make any more mistakes this time.

Cold realisation swept through him—of what he was doing and how badly he'd allowed his control to slip. She was supposed to trust him, supposed to feel safe with him—that was the whole point. And he wasn't supposed to make any more mistakes.

'You should leave,' he forced out, trying to handle the fury that coursed through him. 'I'm not fit company right now.'

She gave him another of those wary looks, but didn't move. 'Why not?'

'Too much wine, too many women, and not enough song.' He tried to hold on to his usual lazy, casual demeanour, baring his teeth in what he hoped was a smile, but probably wasn't. 'Leave, Leonie. I'm not in the mood to be kind.'

Yet again she made no move, only studied him as if he was a mystery she wanted to unravel and not a man she should be afraid of. A man whose passions ran too hot for anyone's comfort.

'Why?' she asked again. 'What happened?'

His fury wound tighter. He didn't want to talk about this with her and he didn't know why she was even interested. She shouldn't be wanting to know more; she should be running back upstairs to the safety of her room.

'I commend your interest in my wellbeing, *gatita*. But I think it is a mistake.' He moved closer since she wasn't getting the message. 'I'm telling you to leave for a reason.'

She was still pressed up against the bookshelves behind her but, strangely, her earlier alarm seemed to have vanished. Instead she was frowning slightly, searching his face as if looking for something, her gaze full of what looked like…concern, almost.

You've done nothing to deserve it.

No, he hadn't. Not a single damn thing.

Her scent wrapped around him and he was aware that the black T-shirt of her uniform was very fitted, outlining to perfection the soft curves of her breasts. They were round and full, just the right size for his hands. Would they be sensitive if he touched them? If he put his mouth to them? Kissed them and sucked on her nipples? Some women were very sensitive there, the slightest touch making them moan, while others needed firmer handling…

'What reason is that?' Leonie asked, and her sweet husky voice did nothing to halt the flood of sexual awareness coursing through him.

There was no alarm in the question, and her gaze was direct. Almost as if she was challenging him. Which would be either very brave, or very foolish, especially when he was in this kind of mood.

'You don't want to know,' he said roughly. 'It might frighten you.'

A spark glowed suddenly in the depths of her eyes. 'I'm not scared of you.'

It was fascinating, that spark. It burned bright and hot and he couldn't drag his gaze from it. Yes, this time it was definitely a challenge, and all he could think about was the fact that Anna had never looked at him that way. Anna had never challenged him—not once.

'You should be.' His voice had deepened, become even rougher, and his groin tightened in response to her nearness. 'I've told you before. I'm not a kind man.'

'That's a lie.' She gave him another searching look, apparently oblivious to the danger. 'You've been nothing but kind since I got here.'

Naturally she'd think that. She wasn't to know that he was being kind only because he wanted something from her. That he wasn't doing this out of the goodness of his heart, but to appease his own desire for vengeance.

Tell her, then. Tell her so she knows.

But if he told her she might run, and he couldn't afford for her to do that. Not yet.

She might run from you anyway if you keep on like this.

It was true. Which meant he needed to pull himself together—perhaps call one of those women who'd indicated interest tonight. It had been a while since he'd taken anyone to bed, so maybe it was that getting to him. Sex had always been his go-to when it came to working out his more primitive emotions. That was why he revelled in it.

'My kindness has a threshold,' he said instead. 'And you're approaching it.'

Her head tilted, her gaze still bright. Almost as if she was pushing him.

'Why? What have I done? You're not very good at answering questions, are you?'

He should have moved—should have stepped away. Should definitely not still be standing there, so close to her, now he'd decided he was going to find some alternative female company.

Yet he couldn't bring himself to move. He was caught by the bright spark in her eyes and by her sweet scent. There was colour in her cheeks still and the pulse at the base of her throat was beating even faster. Her mouth was full and red. Such temptation.

He could kiss that mouth. He could stop her questions and her ill-considered challenges simply by covering it with his own. Would she taste sweet? As sweet as she smelled?

'You haven't done anything but be where you shouldn't be.' He lifted his hand before he could stop himself and gently brushed her bottom lip with his fingertips. 'Which is a mistake, *gatita.*'

Her mouth was as soft as he'd thought it would be, and velvety like rose petals. She stilled, her eyes going wide. But she didn't pull away.

Aren't you going to find yourself another woman?

He was. So why he wasn't—why he was stand-

ing here and touching *this* woman he had no idea.
It shouldn't matter which woman he touched, and
since Anna he'd made sure it didn't. He didn't need
someone who was his—not again.

Not when you can't be trusted with them.

The thought should have made him move away.
But it didn't. Instead, he put one hand on the bookshelf behind her head, leaning over her while he
dragged the tip of his finger across the softness of
her skin, tracing the line of her lower lip.

She shivered, taking another audible breath, her
gaze never leaving his face. Her body was stiff with
tension and yet she didn't move, the spark in her eyes
leaping higher.

'Why are you touching me?' Her voice had become even huskier than normal.

'Why do you think?'

Every muscle in his body had tightened; his groin
was aching. His anger had dulled. Physical desire
was smoothing the sharp edges and making it less
acute. Replacing it with another, safer hunger.

'This is the reason you should have left, Leonie.'
He dragged his finger gently over her bottom lip
once more, pressing against the full softness of it.
'Because you're a lovely woman and I'm a very, *very*
bad man.'

Leonie couldn't move. Or rather, she probably
could—it was more that she didn't want to. And she
didn't understand why, because what the duke was

doing to her should have sent her bolting from the room in search of her knife.

A week ago it would have.

But that had been before she'd spent a whole week in his house, cleaning the rooms she'd been assigned to. A whole week of a comfortable bed and good food, of being clean and dry and warm. A whole week of being safe.

A whole week of him stopping by every day to visit her—sometimes just to say hello, sometimes to chat.

She hadn't realised how much she liked his little visits until the fourth day, when he hadn't stopped by the room she was cleaning and she'd begun to feel annoyed, wondering if she'd missed him. Wondering if she'd been forgotten.

If she'd still been the Leonie of a week ago being forgotten would have been preferable. But she wasn't that Leonie. Not since she'd fallen asleep in his study that night and he'd gathered her up in his arms and put her to bed.

She'd woken the next morning disorientated and restless, panicking slightly when she'd realised what had happened. But when she'd jerked back the quilt she'd found she was still fully clothed. Only her shoes had been removed. She'd been asleep, at her most vulnerable, and all he'd done was tuck her into bed.

Perhaps that was why she felt no fear now, even though he was definitely touching her and threatening her into the bargain. But it wasn't a threat like those she'd experienced before, that promised only violence and pain. No, this was different. This promised something else, and she wasn't at all sure she wouldn't like whatever it was he was promising.

Especially if it was this prickling kind of heat sweeping over her, making her mouth feel full and sensitive. Making something inside her pulse hard and low, with that same hunger she'd felt the night he'd gripped her wrist.

Unfamiliar feelings. Good feelings.

She didn't want to move in case they vanished, as everything good in her life always seemed to do.

She tipped her head back against the bookshelf, staring up him, right into those intense green eyes. There was a flame burning there, giving out more heat than the fire that night in his study, and she wanted more of it. More of the heat of his tall, powerful body so close to hers.

Men had never been anything but threatening to her before, and sex something only offered as a transaction or taken with violence. She knew that there was more to it than that, because she'd watched couples holding hands in the streets. Couples hugging. Couples kissing.

She'd once been interrupted by a well-dressed man and woman slipping into the alley she'd been sleeping in at the time, and had watched unseen from behind a pile of boxes as the man had gently pressed the woman to the brick wall of the alley and lifted her dress. The woman had moaned, but not in protest. Her hands had clutched at the man, pulling him to her, and when she'd cried out it hadn't been in pain.

Leonie had wondered what it would be like to be that woman, but she knew she never would be. Because to be that woman she'd have to be clean and wear a nice dress. To be that woman she'd have to be cared for, and the only person who'd ever cared for her was herself.

So, since physical pleasure was not for people like her, she'd had to settle on invisibility instead. Blending into the background and never calling attention to herself, staying unnoticed and unseen, the way her mother had always taught her.

Except she wasn't unseen now. The duke had seen her, and continued to see her, and with every brush of his finger he made her more and more visible. More and more aware of how she liked that touch, how she wanted it. How cold she'd been before, and also how lonely.

And now he was here, with his hot green eyes and his hard, muscular body, and he was touching her.

He was turning her into that woman in the pretty dress in the alley and she liked it. She didn't want to run away. She wanted to be that woman. The woman who deserved pleasure and who got it.

'I don't think you're bad.' She held his gaze, every nerve-ending she had focused on the touch of his finger on her mouth. 'If you were that bad you wouldn't have told me to leave.'

'I don't think you know bad men, in that case.'

His gaze was all-consuming, a dark forest full of secrets, making her want to journey into it, discover what those secrets were.

'Of course I do.' Her mouth felt achingly sensitive. His touch was so light it was oddly maddening. 'I see them all the time on the streets. And I avoid them whenever I can.'

'So why aren't you running now?'

He shifted, leaning a fraction closer, bracing himself on the bookshelf behind her while his fingers moved on her mouth, his thumb pressing gently on her lip as if testing it.

'Or perhaps it's because you can't see past a warm bed and good food.'

That could be true. He might have lulled her into a false sense of security. She'd been wrong a couple of times before. But she didn't think she was wrong now. He'd had plenty of opportunity to touch her, to take what he wanted, and he hadn't. He had no reason to do so now.

Yes, so why now?

Good point. His obvious sexual interest was rather sudden. Perhaps he didn't want her the way she thought he did. Perhaps he was only trying to frighten her away.

After all, he'd been in a strange mood when he'd come in, with a sharp, raw energy to him, his eyes glittering like shards of green glass. Anger, she was sure, though she wasn't sure why.

Perhaps he'd come into the library hoping for some time to himself and found her there instead, intruding. Ignoring him when he told her to leave. And now he'd had to take more drastic steps to scare her off.

He doesn't want you, idiot. Why would he?

Her stomach dipped, an aching disappointment filling her. There was no reason for him to want her. She was just a homeless person he'd rescued from the streets and for some reason been kind to. And because she hadn't taken the hint and left when he'd asked her to he'd had to be more explicit. All this touching and getting close to her wasn't actually about *her*, and she'd be an idiot to think otherwise.

She tore her gaze away, not wanting him to see her disappointment or the hurt that had lodged inside her. 'Perhaps you're right. Perhaps you're really not all that kind after all.' She tried to sound as level as she could. 'If you want me to go, you'd better move.'

Yet the hard, masculine body crowding her against the bookshelves didn't move. She stared at the fine white cotton of his shirt—he was in evening clothes tonight, so it was obvious he'd been to some fancy party or other—her heartbeat thudding in her ears, a sick feeling in her gut.

Then the finger stroking her mouth dropped, as did the arm near her ear, and the duke straightened up, giving her some room.

The feeling of disappointment deepened.

She pushed herself away from the bookshelf,

wanting to get away now, to get some distance from him. But before she could go past him, his fingers closed around her upper arm.

Her bare upper arm.

Leonie froze. His fingers burned against her skin the way they had that night in his study, making her breath catch and that restless heat sweep over her yet again.

She didn't look at him, staring straight ahead, her pulse racing. 'I thought you wanted me to go?'

'I thought I did, too.' His voice was dark, with threads of heat winding through it. 'You're really not scared of me, are you?'

'Does it matter?' She tried not to shiver in response to the sound of his voice, though it was difficult. 'I'm sorry I was here when you came in. I know you wanted to be alone, and I shouldn't—'

His fingers tightened around her arm abruptly and she broke off.

'Why did you think I wanted to be alone?' he demanded.

'You looked angry, and I shouldn't have been in here.'

'You're fine to be in here. Also, yes, it does matter.'

His fingers felt scorching. 'You should let me go.' She kept her gaze on the wall opposite, trying to ignore his heat and the delicious scent of his aftershave. 'I know you were trying to scare me away—but, for the record, it won't work.'

There was a tense silence, full of the same humming tension that had surrounded them last week in his study.

'It won't, hmm…?'

Unexpectedly, his thumb stroked the underside of her arm in a caress that sent goosebumps scattering all over her skin. 'That's something you shouldn't have told me.'

'Why not?'

'Because it only makes me want try harder to scare you, of course.'

The sound of her heart hammered in her ears. She stared blindly across the room, every sense she possessed concentrated on the man standing beside her, holding her.

Was that another warning? And if it was, why was he still holding her? If he really wanted her to leave he only needed to open his hand and she'd be free.

Yet he hadn't.

She tried to process what that meant, but it was difficult when his thumb was pressing against the sensitive flesh of her under-arm, caressing lightly.

You could pull away. You don't have to stand here.

That was true. She didn't need to stand there being reminded of how empty and cold her life was, of all the good things she was missing out on. She didn't need to be reminded of how unwanted and unneeded she was.

Anyway, she had a warm bed, and food, and a

job. Wanting more than that was just being greedy. She should be happy with what she had.

'All this talk of scaring me and being bad—yet you're not doing anything but hold on to me.' She kept her gaze resolutely ahead. 'I know you don't really want me. So why don't you just be done with it and let me go?'

There was a moment of silence and then she was being tugged around to face him, his glittering green gaze clashing with hers.

'What on earth makes you think I don't want you?' he demanded.

'Why would you?' She lifted her chin, prepared for the truth, ignoring the hurt lodged deep inside her. 'I'm just some poor homeless woman you picked up from the streets. No one else has ever wanted me so why should you?'

The hot flame in his eyes leapt, an emotion she couldn't name flickering over his handsome face. *'Gatita...'*

He looked as if he might say something more, but he didn't. Instead he jerked her suddenly towards him.

Not expecting it, she flung up her hands, her palms connecting with the heat and hardness of his broad chest. His fingers had curled around both her upper arms now, keeping her prisoner, and he'd bent his head, so his green eyes were all she could see.

'You are very foolish indeed if you think that,' he said, in a soft, dangerous voice.

Then, before she could say anything more, his mouth covered hers.

She froze in shock. She'd never been kissed before—had never wanted to be. Although sometimes, when the nights were very dark and she was especially cold, she'd remember that man and woman in the alleyway. Remember how the woman had cried out and how the man had kissed her, silencing her. And she'd wonder what it would feel like to have someone's mouth touching hers. Kissing her...

Now she knew. And it became very clear why that woman had clutched at the man kissing her.

The duke's lips were warm, so much softer than she'd expected a man's lips to be, and the subtle pressure and implicit demand were making a river of unfamiliar heat course the length of her spine.

She trembled, curling her fingers into the warm cotton of his shirt, her own mouth opening beneath his almost automatically. And he took advantage, his tongue pushing inside, tasting her, coaxing her, beginning to explore her.

A low, helpless moan escaped her. The delicious flavour of him was filling her senses and making her want more. She clutched at his shirt tighter, pressing herself closer. The heat of his kiss was melting all the frozen places inside her. All the lonely places. Lighting up all the dark corners of her soul.

Her awareness narrowed on the heat of his mouth, the slow exploration of his tongue, the dark, rich flavour that was all him and the iron-hard body she was pressed against.

It was overwhelming.

It was not enough.

It was everything she'd missed out on, all the good things she'd never had, and now she'd had a taste she wanted more.

She wanted them all.

'Cristiano…' she murmured against his mouth. And the name he'd given her, that she'd only used once before now, came out of her as easily as breathing. 'Please…'

CHAPTER SIX

HE SHOULDN'T HAVE kissed her. Yet now her mouth was open beneath his, the sweet taste of her was on his tongue and the slender heat of her body was pressed against him, he couldn't stop.

She was right in thinking he'd been trying to scare her. And he'd expected it to be easy—that a blatantly sexual touch would have her jerking away from him and leaving the room.

But she hadn't run as he'd anticipated. Because it seemed she never did the thing he anticipated.

Instead she'd only stayed where she was and let him touch her. Let his fingers trace her soft mouth, looking up at him, her eyes darkening with what could only be arousal.

He should have let her go. He hadn't needed to keep holding on to her and he wasn't sure why he had. He certainly shouldn't have compounded his mistake by covering her mouth with his—not when he'd already decided that he wasn't going to have her.

But something in his heart had stopped him. Because the way she'd looked so defiantly up at him, telling him that no one had ever wanted her before and why should he... Well, he hadn't been able to stand it.

A kiss to prove her wrong—that was all it was supposed to be. A kiss to ease the hurt she hadn't been able to hide. And maybe, too, a kiss to frighten her away once and for all.

No, you kissed her because you wanted to, because you wanted her.

Whatever the reason, it didn't matter. What did matter was the furnace that had roared to life inside him the minute her mouth was under his. The very second he'd felt her soften and melt against him, a throaty, husky moan escaped her.

And he wasn't sure why, or what it was about her that had got him burning hot and instantly hard. Yet as she arched against him, her fingers tugging on his shirt, the desire that just about strangled him was as if he hadn't had a woman in months. Years, even.

He could taste her desperation, could feel it in the way she pressed against him, in the sound of his name whispered in her husky voice, so erotic it felt as if she'd reached inside his trousers and wrapped her fingers directly around his shaft.

Anna had never done any of those things during sex. She'd never clutched at him, never moaned his name or pressed herself against him. She'd found his brand of earthy, physical sexuality uncomfortable, telling him he was too demanding. He'd tried to be less so, restraining himself to make her comfortable, turning sex from something passionate into something softer, more palatable, and thus more acceptable. Though it still hadn't been enough for her.

Since she'd left, and since his son had been claimed by another, he'd lost his taste for passion. Something easy, fun and pleasurable—that was all he wanted from sex, nothing more. His lovers could touch his body but they touched nothing else, and that was the way he made sure it always was.

But there was something about the way Leonie clutched at his shirt, her mouth open and hungry beneath his, whispering his name against his lips, that reached inside him, unleashing something he'd kept caged for a long time.

Raw, animal passion.

Perhaps it was because she wasn't a random woman he'd met at a party, or some pretty socialite he'd picked up at a bar. A woman who didn't want more from him than one night and a couple of orgasms, and that was all.

Perhaps it was the wrongness of it. Because there were so many reasons why it was a bad idea. She'd been living on the streets. She was homeless. She was a virgin. She was the daughter of his enemy and he was going to use her to get his revenge. He should not be hard for her, let alone kissing her hungrily late at night in his study.

And yet when she whispered, 'Cristiano… Please…' and arched against him, the soft curves of her breasts pressing against his chest, the sound of his name spoken in her husky voice echoing in his ears, all he could think about was giving her exactly what she was begging for.

After all, who was he to deny her? He'd never been a man to refuse anyone when it came to sex, still less one bright and beautiful woman whom he wanted very much.

Besides, perhaps taking her would cement what trust there was between them rather than break it. And when desire was this strong it was always better not to fight it. Always better to take command and sate it so it was easier to control later on.

That all sounds like some excellent justification.

But Cristiano was done listening to his better self.

He dropped his hands from her upper arms to her hips, letting them rest there a second to get her used to his touch. Then he slid them higher, until his palms were gently cupping her breasts.

She gave another of those delicious little moans, shuddering and then arching into his hands like a cat wanting to be stroked. He kept his mouth on hers, making the kiss teasing as he traced her soft curves with his fingertips before brushing his thumbs over the hard outlines of her nipples.

She gasped and he wanted to devour her whole, but he forced himself to lift his mouth from hers instead, to stare down into her face to check if she was still with him. Her cheeks were deeply flushed, her lips full and red from the kiss.

'Why did you stop?' she asked breathlessly. 'Please don't.'

Oh, yes, she was with him.

Satisfaction pulsed through him and he took her mouth again, nipping at her bottom lip at the same time as he pinched her nipples lightly, making her jerk and shudder against him.

His own heartbeat roared in his ears; his groin was aching. He wanted her naked, wanted her skin bare to his touch, wanted her hands on him, clutching at him. He wanted her desperate for him.

He'd given her food and drink. Given her a job. Given her a bed. And now he wanted to give her pleasure, too. He didn't pause to examine why this was important to him—he just wanted to.

Dangerous. You know how you get when you give in to your passions.

Ah, but this was only sex. It wouldn't touch his emotions in any way. He'd make sure of it.

'Gatita,' he murmured roughly against her hungry mouth. 'In ten seconds I'm going to have you naked on the floor, so if that's not what you want you'd better tell me right now.'

'I want it.' There was no hesitation in her voice, no coy dancing around the subject. 'Cristiano, please—I want it.'

Desire soaked through every husky word, and when he lifted his head and looked down into her eyes a part of him was shocked by the nakedness of her desire. Because she made no effort to hide it.

Everything she felt was laid bare for him to see, exposing a vulnerability he was sure she hadn't meant to expose.

He could use that against her if he chose—get her to do anything he wanted if he handled it right. Even convince her to be his wife, for example. And if he'd been a more unscrupulous man...

What are you talking about? You are an unscrupulous man.

Oh, he was. But there was something innocent about Leonie, an honesty that he found almost painful. And he could not bring himself to take advantage of it.

Though she should know better than to let herself be so vulnerable—especially with a man like him. He was dangerous and hadn't he told her that? She needed to be more wary, more on her guard.

He bent his head further, moving his mouth to her jaw, kissing down the side of her neck and nipping her again in sensual punishment. But, again, she didn't push him away, only pulled harder on his shirt instead, as if she wanted more.

It was like petrol being poured over an already blazing fire, making his own passion leap high and hot.

Without another word, he lifted her into his arms and carried her over to the soft silk rug in front of the empty fireplace. Then he laid her down on it and took the hem of her T-shirt in his hands, dragging it up and over her head.

She didn't stop him, and a wave of gorgeous pink swept down her throat and over her chest as he uncovered her. The colour turned her eyes a vivid blue and made the plain black bra she wore stand out. But not for long. He undid the catch and stripped that from her, too, leaving her upper body bare.

Instantly her hands went to cover herself, but he caught her wrists, preventing her. 'No,' he said roughly, unable to keep his voice level. 'I want to look at you.'

She swallowed, but there was no resistance in her as he pushed her down onto her back, taking her arms above her head and pinning them to the rug, gripping her crossed wrists in one hand.

Lying there stretched out beneath him, all silky pale skin, her breasts exposed, hard nipples flushed a deep pink, she was the most delectable thing he'd ever seen.

He stared down into her eyes, watching the passion that burned there burn even higher as he stroked his free hand up and down her sides.

'Cristiano…' she said breathlessly, shivering.

'What it is, *gatita*? Do you need more?' He moved his hand to cup one of those perfect breasts, felt her skin hot against his palm. 'This, perhaps?'

'Oh…' she sighed. 'That's so—'

She broke off on a gasp as he rubbed his thumb over one hard nipple before pinching it, watching the pleasure chase itself over her lovely face. Her body arched beneath his hand, her lashes half closing.

'Oh…that's so good. More…'

His little kitten was demanding.

Yours? Already?

Maybe. And why not? No one else had claimed her, so why couldn't he? She was so very responsive, so very rewarding. Making her gasp like that might even become addictive.

He pinched her again, rolling her nipple between his thumb and forefinger, making her writhe. 'You'd best be more respectful,' he murmured, teasing the tip of her breast relentlessly. 'Please and thank you are always welcome.'

'Please…' She moaned softly, arching yet again beneath him. 'Please, more…'

'So obedient.' He eased his hand lower, over the soft skin of her stomach to the fastening of her plain black trousers. 'I like that, though. I like how you beg for me.'

Flicking open the button of her trousers, he grabbed the zip and drew it down. Then he pushed his hand beneath the fabric and over the front of her underwear. She shuddered as his fingers traced her through the damp cotton, pleasure and a certain wonder making her eyes glow. She was looking at him as though he'd shown her something amazing, the most precious thing in all the universe.

'Oh…' Her eyes went very wide as he pressed a finger gently against the most sensitive part of her and then circled around it, making her hips shudder and lift. 'What are you doing?' She didn't sound alarmed, only a little shocked.

'Giving you pleasure.' His voice came out rougher than he'd intended. 'Does it feel good, Leonie? Does it feel good when I touch you?'

'Yes, oh, yes…' The breath sighed out of her and her gaze fixed to his, more wonder and amazement in her eyes. 'I never thought…it would…feel like this.'

She was so unguarded, so sincere. This woman had been denied a lot of things—warmth and comfort and safety. She'd been denied physical pleasure, too, and that was a crime. Because it was becoming apparent to him that she was a creature of passion, greedy for all the pleasure he could give her. And he had a lot of that to give.

Pleasure wasn't new to him, but for some reason introducing her to it was completely addictive. From the way she shivered under his hand to the flush in her silky skin. From the sounds she made to the wonder of discovery as she looked at him.

It was a discovery for him as well, he realised. It had been a long time since he'd been engaged in bed. He always gave his partners pleasure, but only in so far as it affected his own reputation. It was never about the woman in particular.

But now it was about this woman. He wanted to give her something she'd never had before—wanted to show her something new. He wanted her to look at him exactly the way she was looking at him now, as if she'd never seen anything or anyone so amazing in all her life.

The way no one, not even Anna, had ever looked at him.

You can't give that up.

A dark, ferocious thing stretched out lazily inside him, flexing its claws.

Well, maybe he didn't have to give it up. Why should he? She wanted him—that was obvious—and passion like hers didn't stay sated. This needn't be a one-off thing. He was planning on marrying her anyway, so why not make it a true marriage for a time?

Are you sure that's a good idea? Look what happened last time with Anna.

Yes, but that had only been because those dangerous emotions of his had been involved, and they weren't here. He didn't love Leonie and she didn't love him. He was simply taking advantage of their intense physical chemistry, nothing more.

She might not feel that way when you tell her you've known who she is all along.

Cristiano ignored that thought, slipping his hand beneath the fabric of her underwear, then sliding his fingers over her slick, wet flesh. She gave a little cry, pushing herself into his touch, her eyes darkening as her pupils dilated.

Satisfaction deepened inside him. He could have watched the pleasure rippling over her face for ever. 'You like that, *mi corazón*? Do you like it when I stroke you here?'

He found the small, sensitive bud between her thighs and brushed the tip of his finger over and around it. She gasped, shivering.

'And here?'

He shifted his hand, put his thumb where his finger had been, then slid that finger down through the slick folds of her sex to the entrance of her body, easing gently inside.

'Do you like it when I touch you here?'

Her cheeks were deeply flushed and she moved restlessly, unable to keep still. 'Yes…' Her voice had become even more hoarse. 'Oh, yes… Cristiano… I need…'

He could become addicted to hearing his name spoken like that…husky and soft and desperate. Just as he could become addicted to the silky, slippery feel of her flesh and the hot grip of her body around his finger. To the way she shook and gasped and arched. To the obvious pleasure she was feeling and didn't hide.

His groin was aching, his own desire winding tight, and he wanted to be inside her with a desperation he hadn't thought possible.

But he wanted to watch her come even more. So he eased his fingers in and out of her, adding more pressure and friction with his thumb until her eyes went wide and her mouth opened and her body convulsed.

She cried out in shocked pleasure as her climax hit, and he leaned down and kissed her, tasting that pleasure for himself.

* * *

Cristiano's mouth on hers was so hot and so delicious she could hardly bear it. Waves of the most intense pleasure were shaking her, and all she could do was lie there and let them wash over her.

She'd told him the truth when she'd said she'd had no idea it would feel like this. She really hadn't. Had the woman against that wall felt the same pleasure? Was it this that had made her cry out? Because, yes, *now* she understood. Now she got it completely.

When Cristiano had touched her she'd felt as if something was blooming inside her. A flower she'd thought had died, which had turned out to be only dormant, waiting for the sun, and now the sun was shining and she was opening up to it, revelling in it.

She hadn't been afraid. His kiss had been hot but his hands gentle, and when a fit of modesty had overcome her when he'd taken her bra off he'd been very clear that he wanted to look at her. That he liked looking at her.

And so she'd let him. And the longer he'd looked, the more she'd wanted him to. Because she'd seen the effect she'd had on him, the heat burning in his eyes, and it had made her feel…beautiful. She'd never felt that before, nor ever been conscious of her own feminine power. Her ability to make him burn as much as he made her.

Then he'd touched her, and the world around her had turned to fire.

Perhaps she should be ashamed that she'd been

so open with her responses. Perhaps she should have been more guarded. But the pleasure had been too intense, and she simply hadn't been able to hide her feelings.

He'd touched her as if she wasn't some dirty forgotten kid that he'd found on the streets of Paris. He'd touched her as if she was precious...as if she was worth something. He'd touched her as if he cared about her, and she realised that she wanted him to.

It didn't make any sense—not when she hadn't known him long—yet every touch had only made her more certain. He'd given her many things she'd been missing in her life and now he was giving her another—something she'd never thought she'd want.

And, despite the fact that he'd seemed so angry when he'd come into the library earlier, he wasn't taking that anger out on her. He wasn't taking from her at all.

He was giving to her. Giving heat and a shivery desperation. A delicious need. Pleasure to chase away the cold and the dark, the fear and the loneliness. So much pleasure...

She wanted more of it.

She tried to pull her hands away from his restraining hold, but his grip only firmed as his glittering green eyes scanned her from head to foot.

'Are you okay?'

His voice was a soft, roughened caress, whispering over her skin like velvet.

'Did you like that?'

'Yes. Very much.' She didn't sound much better herself. 'But I want you. I want to touch you.'

There was no hiding it so she didn't bother.

He swept his free hand down the length of her body in a long stroke that soothed her at the same time as it excited her.

'There will be time for that. But first, you're wearing far too many clothes.'

With practiced, careful hands he stripped the rest of the clothing from her body, finally baring her.

She'd thought she might feel terribly vulnerable and exposed, being naked in front of a man. Being naked in front of anyone, really. But she didn't feel either of those things. Only strangely powerful as he pulled the fabric away from her and she saw the look on his face became hungrier, sharper, as if the sight of her was something he'd been waiting lifetimes for.

And when she was finally naked, lying back on the rug, he knelt over her, his gaze roaming all over her body, and she felt for the first time in her life as if maybe there was something worthwhile about her after all.

What it was, she didn't know. But it was certainly something that had this powerful duke looking at her as if she was the Holy Grail itself.

He ran his fingertips lightly all over her, inciting her, watching her face as he did so, gauging her every response as if there was nothing more important in the world than discovering which touches made her shiver and which made her moan. Which ones made her pant his name.

She'd long since lost any shyness by the time he pushed apart her legs, brushing his mouth over her trembling stomach before moving further down. And then all she could do was thread her fingers in his hair as he put that clever mouth of his between her thighs.

Pleasure exploded through her as he began to explore, his fingers delicately parting her wet flesh while his tongue licked and caressed, driving her higher and higher. Making her cry out as the most delicious ecstasy threaded through her.

She'd never thought this feeling would be hers. Never thought that sex could be something so intense, so incredible, that it would feel so good. She'd never thought it would make her feel treasured and desired rather than dirty and worthless, but with every flick of his tongue and stroke of his hand that was what he made her feel.

She pulled on his hair, crying his name as he pushed his tongue inside her and she shattered for a second time, her climax so all-consuming that all she could do was lie there with her eyes closed as it washed over her, feeling him stroke her gently as he moved away.

Then there came the rustle of clothing and the sound of a zip being drawn down, the crinkle of foil. And then the brush of hot skin on hers, setting every nerve-ending to aching life once again.

She opened her eyes.

The duke was kneeling between her spread thighs, tall, powerful and extremely naked. And somehow he seemed even more intimidating without his clothes on, because all that lazy amusement, the studied air of ennui, had vanished completely as if it had never been.

It was a smokescreen, she realised. A distraction. A disguise hiding the true nature of the man beneath it.

She'd imagined him as a panther, lazily sunning himself on a branch, and he was that. But a panther was a predator—and that was what she was looking at now, not the lazy cat.

He was all velvet tanned skin drawn over sharply defined muscle, broad and powerful and strong. A work of art. A Greek statue come to life. As hard as the bronze from which he'd been fashioned yet not cold, but hot. Heated metal and oiled silk.

And his beautiful face was drawn tight with hunger and intent. His eyes had narrowed; hot emerald was glittering from between silky black lashes. The panther ready to pounce. The predator ready to feast.

A delicious shiver chased over her body and she allowed herself to look down to where he was hot and hard and ready for her. She'd never thought that could be beautiful as well, but it was. She pushed herself up on one hand and reached to touch him, and he made no move to stop her, letting her fingers brush along the velvet-smooth skin of his shaft.

She looked up at his face as she did it, wanting to see what effect her touch had on him, and was thrilled to see a muscle jump in the side of his impressive jaw.

'No playing, *gatita*,' he murmured, his rich voice dark and thick with heat. 'Like I said, my patience is limited.'

'I want to touch you, though.' She closed her fingers around him, marvelling at how hard he was and yet how soft and smooth his skin felt. 'You're so hard...' She squeezed experimentally.

He hissed, and then suddenly everything was moving very quickly. He pulled her hand away and pushed her down on her back, his long, muscular body settling over hers. She protested, but he shook his head, the smile he gave her sharp and edged.

'You can touch me later. Seems I have limited patience where you are concerned.'

She liked that. Liked the way her touch could incite him the way his could incite her.

She wanted to help him with the protection, too, but he gave a sharp shake of his head, dealing with it himself. And then his hands were sliding beneath her bottom, gripping her tight and lifting her, and he was positioning himself so he was pressing gently at her entrance.

'Are you ready for me?'

His jaw was set and hard, every muscle in his body drawn tight and ready. All that strength and power was held back, and not without effort. But it was definitely held back. For her.

'Answer me. I'm not made of stone.'

What a lie. He *was* made of stone. Not bronze after all, but hard, living rock that she couldn't stop touching. Enduring and powerful. She could shelter beneath him right here and nothing would touch her.

The feeling was so intense she put her hands on his chest and spread out her fingers, stroking up over all that hard muscle to his strong shoulders. Holding on.

'I'm ready,' she whispered.

And he didn't hesitate, his fingers tightening as he pushed into her. She gasped as she felt her flesh part for him, in an intense yet delicious stretch, and tensed, ready for pain, because this was supposed to hurt. Yet apart from a slight pinch there was nothing. Only more of that sensual stretch that had her panting and twisting in his arms as she tried to adjust to the sensation.

'Look at me,' he ordered. 'Look at me, Leonie.'

So she did, staring straight up into his eyes, and suddenly everything clicked into place. She was made for him. Her body was made especially for him—for his hands and his mouth, for the hard, male part of him, and he was where he was supposed to be. He might be holding her, but she was also holding him.

'Cristiano…' She lingered over the sound of it, loving how it felt to say it. Loving, too, the way his eyes flared as she said it. So she said it again, digging her nails into his skin, lifting her hips, because she was ready for him to move. Ready for him to take her on another journey.

'Demanding, *gatita*,' he growled. 'You are perfect.'

Then he covered her mouth in a kiss so hot and blinding she trembled and he began to move, the long, lazy glide of him inside her making more of that intense, delicious pleasure sweep over her.

She tried to press herself harder against him, because it wasn't quite enough and she didn't know how to get more, and then he reached down and hooked one hand behind her knee, drawing her leg up and around his hip, allowing him to sink deeper, and she moaned in delight against his mouth.

He felt so good. The glide of his hips, the silk of his skin, the flex and release of all those powerful muscles as he thrust in and out. The warm spice of his scent was cut through with the musk of his arousal. It was delicious.

She sank her teeth into his lower lip, hardly aware of what she was doing, only knowing she wanted even more of him and this insanely pleasurable movement. He growled in response—a deep rumble in his chest that sent chills through her.

Yes, she wanted the panther. The raw untamed part of him, not the lazy, civilised man he was on the outside. Not the smokescreen. Did anyone else know he was this way? Was he like this when he made love to other women?

She didn't like that thought—not at all. She wanted him to be like this with her and only her.

She bit him again, scratching him with her nails, thrilled when he grabbed her hands and held them down on either side of her head.

He lifted his mouth from hers and looked into her eyes as he thrust hard and deep. 'You like showing me your claws, don't you?' He sounded breathless. 'What's that all about, hmm…?'

'You're not the only one who's bad.' She put a growl of her own into her voice as she pulled her hands away, running her nails down his back in a long scratch, lifting her hips to meet his thrust. 'You're not the one who's dangerous.'

'Is that so?' He thrust harder, pushing deeper, making her gasp and arch her back, her nails digging in. 'Show me how bad you are, then, *leona*. Show me your teeth.'

Pleasure twisted inside her and she turned her head, bit his shoulder, tasting the salt and musk of his skin, loving how he gave another growl deep in his throat and moved faster.

She clung to him, licking him, biting him, scratching him as pleasure drew so tight that she didn't think she could bear it. She called his name desperately and he answered, shifting one hand down between them and stroking her where she needed it most. And then she had to turn her face against his neck as everything came apart inside her. Tears flooded her eyes and she was sobbing his name as ecstasy annihilated her.

She had a dim sense of him moving faster, harder, and then she heard his own roar of release, felt his arms coming around her and holding her, his big, hot body over her and around her, inside her.

Protecting her.

CHAPTER SEVEN

CRISTIANO PULLED A shirt on, slowly doing up the buttons, then methodically starting on the cuffs. He stood at the window of his bedroom while he did so, his attention on the garden below, though he wasn't looking at the view.

He was too busy thinking about what he was going to say to the woman still asleep in the bed behind him. His little *gatita*. Though she wasn't really a kitten. Not after last night. Last night he'd discovered she was a lioness, and he had the scratches down his back to prove it.

It would have made him smile if he'd been in a smiling mood, but he wasn't.

There were a number of things he wanted to do, and he couldn't do any of them until he'd told her that he'd known who she was from the moment he'd taken her home. And that he intended to marry her to take his revenge on her father.

She probably wasn't going to take either of those things well.

Are you sure it's wise to tell her now?

He frowned at the garden for a moment, then turned around.

Leonie was curled up in the centre of his bed, her hair a scatter of brilliant red-gold across his white pillows. She was fast sleep, with the sheet falling down off her shoulders a little, revealing pale, milky skin.

Last night she'd felt like pure joy in his hands, passionate and generous and honest. Pleasure had been a discovery and she a fascinated explorer. She'd denied him nothing, taken everything he'd given, and now all he could think about was doing it again. And again and again.

He hadn't had sex like that in years—if ever.

Leonie hadn't found his passion frightening or uncomfortable, the way Anna had. No, she'd demanded it. And then, when he'd given it to her, she'd demanded more.

His groin hardened, and the decision he'd made in the early hours of the morning, when he'd had to get up and have a cold shower so he could sleep, was now a certainty.

He'd take her back to San Lorenzo, his ancestral estate. There he would have her all to himself. He could certainly tell her about his plans here, but perhaps it would be better if she was at home in Spain. Where he could keep an eye on her.

The chances of her running away or not wanting anything to do with him once she found out about his plans were slim—or so he anticipated—but it was better to be safe than sorry.

Plus, marrying her in the ancient Velazquez family chapel would no doubt rub further salt in the wound for Victor de Riero. A further declaration of Cristiano's possession.

And if she refuses to marry you?

He would just ensure that she wouldn't. Everyone had a price, and no doubt so did she.

Finishing with his cuffs, he moved over to the bed and bent, stroking his fingers along one bare shoulder, smiling as she shivered. Her red-gold lashes fluttered and then she let out a small sigh, rolling over onto her back. The sheet fell all the way to her waist, exposing those small, perfect breasts and their little pink nipples.

He was very tempted to taste one of them, to make her gasp the way he had the night before. But that wouldn't get them any closer to San Lorenzo, and now he'd decided to go he saw no reason to linger in Paris.

'Wake up, sleepy *gatita*,' he murmured, unable to stop himself from brushing his fingers over one pert nipple, watching as it hardened, feeling his own hunger tighten along with it.

She sighed and lifted her arms, giving such a sensual stretch he almost changed his plans right there and then in favour of staying a few more hours in bed with her.

Her eyes opened, deep violet this morning, and she smiled. It took his breath away.

'Good morning.' Her gaze dropped down his body before coming to his face again. 'You're dressed. That's unfortunate.'

He smiled, the beast inside him stretching again, purring in pleasure at her blatant stare. 'Hold that thought. I have plans for us today.'

'What plans?' Her eyes widened and she sat up suddenly. 'What's the time? Am I late for work? Where are my—?'

'There will be no work for you today. Or perhaps any other day.'

He saw shock, hurt and anger ripple across her lovely face. 'Why not? I thought I—'

'Relax, *mi corazón*. I have another position in mind for you.' He sat on the side of the bed and reached for her small hand, holding it in his. 'I'm planning to return to my estate in Spain.'

'Oh.' Her expression relaxed. And then she frowned. 'Why?'

Naturally she would have questions. She was nothing if not curious.

'I have some things that need attention and I haven't been back for a while.'

Years, in reality. Fifteen of them, to be exact. But she didn't need to know that.

He turned her hand over in his, stroking her palm with his thumb. 'It would please me very much to take you with me.'

She glanced down at her hand, enclosed in his. 'But what about my job here? Camille wouldn't like it if I suddenly left with no word.' Another troubled expression crossed her face. 'She wouldn't like it if she knew what I...what we...'

'Leave Camille to me.' He stroked her palm reassuringly, noting how she shivered yet again. 'And, like I told you, I have another position in mind for you.'

She looked up at him, her gaze very direct. 'What position? Your lover?'

There was a challenging note in her voice and he couldn't help but like how unafraid she was to confront him. She was strong, that was for certain, and although she might have been an innocent when it came to sex, she wasn't an innocent in anything else. She'd lived for years on the streets. She would have seen all kinds of cruel things, seen the basest of human nature. She knew how the world worked and knew that it was not kind.

If you tell her the truth she'll understand. She, more than anyone, will know what it's like to lose everything.

It was true. And if she didn't—well, there was always the money option. Either way, it wouldn't be an issue.

'Is there a problem with that?' he asked casually. 'You seemed to enjoy it well enough last night.'

She glanced down once again at her hand resting

in his, at his thumb stroking gently her palm. 'So will that now be my job?'

The question sounded neutral, but he knew it wasn't.

'To be your whore?' The word was like a stone thrown against glass, jagged and sharp. 'Will you pay me more to be in your bed, Cristiano?'

The question sounded raw in the silence of the room. It wasn't a simple challenge now, because there was something else in her tone. She sounded...vulnerable, and he had the sense that he'd hurt her somehow.

You have hurt her.

Anger twisted sharply inside him and he dropped her hand and pushed himself off the bed, striding restlessly over to the window, trying to get his thoughts in order and his ridiculous emotions safely under control again.

The issue, of course, was that she was right. That was exactly what he'd been planning to do. Pay her to be his wife. And since he was also thinking their marriage would include sex, essentially he was paying her to sleep with him.

'Would that be so very bad?' he asked harshly.

There was a brief silence, and then she said in a small voice, 'So that's all last night was? Just a...a transaction?'

Ah, so that was what this was about. She thought the sex had meant something.

It did.

No—and he couldn't afford it to. His emotions had to remain detached, and already they were more engaged than he wanted them to be. His anger was far too close to the surface and she had an ability to rouse it too easily. He had to make sure he stayed uninvolved—that his feelings for her didn't go beyond physical lust.

'I thought last night was all about mutual pleasure,' he said, keeping his tone neutral. 'Though if there was anything transactional about it I apologise.'

'Oh.' Her voice sounded even smaller. 'I see.'

Cristiano's jaw tightened. He hadn't thought about her feelings and he should have. Because of course the sex for her wouldn't simply have been physical. It had been her first time, and she didn't have the experience to tell the difference between great sex and an emotional connection.

Are you sure you do?

He shoved that thought away—hard. Oh, he knew the difference. He wasn't a boy any more. But he couldn't have her thinking that the sex between them had meant more than it had. He also couldn't have her getting under his skin the way she was currently doing.

Which left him with only one option.

He would have to give her the truth.

It would hurt her, but maybe that would be a good thing. Then she would know exactly what kind of man he was. Which was definitely not the kind of man she could have sex that meant something with.

She might not want to have anything to do with you after that.

His chest tightened with a regret and disappointment he didn't want to feel, so he ignored it, placing his hands on the sill and staring sightlessly at the rooftops of Paris.

'I was married years ago,' he said into the silence. 'Both of us were very young—too young, as it turned out. She found me…difficult. And I *was* difficult. But I didn't know that she was so unhappy.' He paused, the words catching unexpectedly in his throat. 'At least not until she left me for someone else.'

Leonie was silent behind him.

'That someone else was an old enemy of my family's,' he went on. 'Someone who befriended me after my parents died and became a mentor to me. I told him about my marriage difficulties in the hope that he'd give me some advice, and he did. All the while using what I said to seduce my wife away from me.'

His grip on the sill tightened, his nails digging into the paintwork.

'And that's not all. I didn't realise that Anna was pregnant when she left me for him. In fact, I only found out when he came to tell me that not only was the baby mine, but he'd organised it so that legally he was the baby's father. I could never claim him.'

There was a soft, shocked sound from behind him, but he ignored it.

'This enemy was a powerful man,' he said

roughly, 'and even though I tried to uncover what he'd done I was unable to. I was young and had no influence, no power and no money.'

He paused yet again, trying to wrestle the burning rage that ate away at him under his control again.

'I felt I had no choice. If I wanted my son I would have to take him by force. And so I planned to do that. I crashed a party they were giving and tried to confront the man who'd taken my child. But I was... angry. So very angry. And I ended up frightening my son. He ran straight into my enemy's arms—'

His voice cracked and he had to fight to keep it level.

'I knew then I had to let him go,' he went on, more levelly this time. 'That I had to let everything go. And so I did.'

Even though it had cut him in half. Even though it had caused his heart to shrivel up and die in his chest.

'I cut my marriage and my son out of my life, out of my memory. I pretended that it never happened, that he never existed. And then...then I found a woman in the streets. A woman who was defacing my car. I found out her name. Leonie de Riero. The long-lost, much-loved daughter of Victor de Riero.'

Cristiano let go of the windowsill and turned around to face the woman in the bed.

'Victor de Riero is the man who first stole my wife and then stole my child from me. And he owes me a debt that I will collect.' He stared at her, let her see the depth of his fury. 'With you.'

* * *

Leonie clutched the sheet tight in her hands, unable to process what Cristiano had just told her.

He stood with the window at his back, his hands at his sides, his fingers curled into fists. His beautiful face was set in hard lines, the look in his emerald eyes so sharp it could cut. The smokescreen had dropped away entirely. He looked fierce, dangerous, and the fury rolling off him took her breath away.

What little breath she had, given that apparently all this time he'd known who she was. Known *exactly* who she was.

That's why he picked you up off the streets. That's why he gave you a job. You were never anything to him but a means to an end.

Pain settled inside her, though she ignored it. As she ignored the cold waves of shock and the sharp tug of pity because there was so much to take in.

He'd been married. He'd had a child. A child that had been taken from him. God, she could still hear his voice cracking as he'd told her what had happened, and that pity tugged harder at her heart.

But she didn't want to feel pity for him.

'You knew,' she said thickly, focusing on that since it was easier than thinking about the rest. 'All this time, you knew.'

His expression was like granite. 'Yes. I went to get my driver and found him playing a dice game with one of your friends. I gave the kids a hundred euros to tell me what your name was.' His mouth quirked in a humourless smile. 'Everyone has their price.'

She felt cold. But it was a cold that came from the inside, something that no amount of blankets or quilts could help. 'But…how could you know who I was from my first name?'

His gaze went to her hair, spilling down her back. 'You were familiar to me and I couldn't put my finger on why. But the colour of your hair gave it away. Anna and I used to go to many events hosted by your father and you attended some of them.'

Her stomach dropped away. Her memories of that time were so dim they were only blurry impressions. A pretty dress. A crowd of adults. Nothing more.

But Cristiano had been there. She must have seen him and clearly he'd remembered her.

She stared at him, her heart pounding. Before, she'd noted that he was older, certainly much older than she was, but she hadn't thought about it again. She hadn't thought about it last night, either—had been too desperate for him.

There had been a vague familiarity to his name when she'd first heard it, but she hadn't remembered anything. She'd been too young.

'Why…?' She stopped, not sure which question to ask first since there were so many.

'Why did I bring you here? Why did I not tell you I knew?' He asked them for her. 'Because you were familiar and I wanted to know why. And when

I discovered who you were I didn't tell you because I wanted you to tell me. I wanted you to trust me.'

A sudden foreboding wound through her. 'What do you want from me?'

He smiled again, his predator's smile, and it chilled her. 'What do I want from you? I want you to help me get my revenge, of course.'

Ice spread through her.

Did you think he wanted you for real?

She fought to think, fought her pity for him and for what had happened to him.

'How? I don't understand.'

'I'm going to marry you, Leonie. And I'm going to invite your father to our wedding, to watch as a Velazquez takes a precious de Riero daughter the way he took my son.'

The ferocity on Cristiano's face, gleaming in his eyes, made the ice inside her deepen, yet at the same time it gave her a peculiar and unwanted little thrill.

'You will be mine, Leonie. And there will be nothing he can do to stop it.'

You want to be someone's.

The thought tangled with all the other emotions knotting in her chest, too many to sort out and deal with. So she tried to concentrate only on the thing that made any kind of sense to her.

'It won't work,' she said. 'My father doesn't care. He left me to rot in the streets.'

Something flickered across Cristiano's intense

features. 'No, he didn't. He thought you were dead. Didn't you know?'

Her stomach dropped away. Dead? He thought she was dead?

'What?' she whispered, hoarse with shock. 'No, my mother told me he got rid of us. That he'd wanted a son, and she couldn't have any more children. And he…he…' She trailed off, because it couldn't be true. It couldn't.

Maybe it is and your mother lied to you.

This time the expression on Cristiano's face was unmistakable: pity.

'He didn't get rid of you,' he said quietly. 'I know. I was there. Your mother left him, and took you with her, and you both disappeared. A week or so later he got word that you'd both died in a fire in Barcelona.'

'No,' she repeated pointlessly. 'No. We came to Paris. Mamá had to get a job. I wanted to go home, but she told me we couldn't because Papá didn't want us. She couldn't give him the son he'd always wanted so he kicked us out.' Leonie took a shaken breath. 'Why would she say that if it wasn't true?'

Cristiano only shook his head. 'I don't know. Perhaps she didn't want you to find out that he'd been having an affair with my wife.'

Does it matter why? She lied to you.

The shock settled inside her, coating all those tangled emotions inside her, freezing them.

'All this time I thought he didn't look for me because he didn't care,' she said thickly. 'But it wasn't that. He thought…he thought I was dead.'

Cristiano's anger had cooled, and a remote expression settled over his face. 'I wouldn't ascribe any tender emotion to him if I were you. He didn't demand proof of your deaths. He merely took some stranger's word for it.'

A lump rose in Leonie's throat. There was a prickling behind her eyes and she felt like crying. Okay, so not only had her father thought she'd died, and hadn't much cared, but her mother had lied to her. Had lied to her for years.

Does knowing all that really change anything?

No, it didn't. She was still homeless. Still in this man's power. This man who'd known who she was all this time and hadn't told her. Who was planning to use her in some kind of twisted revenge plot.

It made her ache, made her furious, that all the heat and passion and wonder of the night before had been a lie. The joy she'd felt as he'd touched her as if she mattered was tainted.

He'd lied to her the way her mother had lied to her.

Bitterness and hurt threatened to overwhelm her, but she grabbed on to that thread of fury. Because fury was easier than pain every single time.

'So that's why you slept with me?' She fought to keep the pain from her voice. 'To make sure I'd do what I was told?'

Something flickered through his green eyes, though she didn't know what it was.

'No, sleeping with you was never the plan. I was going to make sure you trusted me and then I was going to put it to you as a business proposition. If you'd agree to marry me I would pay you a certain amount, and then in a few years we would divorce.'

'I see.' Carefully she drew the sheet around her, though it didn't help the numbness creeping through her. 'The sex was part of building trust, then?'

A muscle flicked in his jaw. 'That wasn't the intention.'

But it was clear that he wasn't unhappy that it had happened between them.

Of course he wasn't. It was another thing for him to use. And you thought you could trust him...

The cold in the pit of her stomach turned sharp, digging in, a jagged pain. She was a fool. The last person she'd trusted had been her mother and look how that had turned out. She'd thought after that she'd be more careful about who she gave her trust to, but apparently she'd learned nothing.

Though, really, what did it matter? The sex had been amazing, but so what? It was only sex and he wasn't different. He was a liar, like everyone else. And one thing was certain: he would never touch her again.

'Then what was your intention?' She was pleased with how level her voice was.

He stared at her for a long moment, his gaze unreadable. 'You're beautiful, Leonie. And I thought—'

'You thought, *Why not? A girl from the streets could be fun? Something a bit different.*'

Bitterness was creeping in now, which wasn't supposed to happen, so she forced it out.

'It doesn't matter,' she went on dismissively. 'It was a nice way to pass the evening.'

Shifting, she slid out of the bed, keeping the sheet wrapped around her as she took a couple of steps towards him, then stopped.

'You didn't need to bother, though. If you'd asked me the night you picked me up if I wanted to help you get revenge on my father I would have said yes. Especially if you're going to pay me.'

Cristiano didn't move, but the line of his shoulders was tense, his jaw tight. His gaze was absolutely impenetrable.

'You have no loyalty to him, then?'

'Why should I? I barely remember him. Money is what I need now.'

There was silence as he stared at her and she couldn't tell what he was thinking.

'For what it's worth,' he said quietly, 'I slept with you last night because you're beautiful and I wanted you, Leonie. Because I couldn't stop myself.'

She hated him a little in that moment, and part of her wanted to throw it back in his face. But that would give away the fact that their night had mattered to her, and she didn't want him to know that. She didn't want him to know *anything*.

Last night she'd trusted him, but she certainly

wasn't going to make that mistake again. His money, on the other hand, was a different story. She could buy herself a new life with money like that. Buy that little cottage in the country, where she'd live with the only person she trusted in the entire world: herself.

So all she did was lift a shoulder as if she didn't care and it didn't matter. 'Fine—but I want the money, Cristiano.'

His features hardened. 'Name your price.'

She thought of the most outrageous sum she could and said it out loud.

'It's yours,' he replied without hesitation.

'There's a condition,' she added.

His granite expression didn't change. 'Which is?'

'You can never touch me again.'

The muscle in the side of his jaw flicked, and there was a steady green glitter in his eyes. 'And if I don't like that condition?'

'Then I'll refuse to help you.'

He said nothing, and didn't move, but she could sense the fury rolling off him in waves. He didn't like her condition. Didn't like it one bit.

'I could make you change your mind.'

The words were more a growl than anything else, and the fighter in her wanted to respond to that challenge, relished it, even.

'Could you?' She gave him a very direct look. 'Why would you bother? I'm just a girl from the streets. You could get better with a snap of your fingers.'

'It's true, I could.' His gaze clashed with hers. 'But I don't want better. I want you.'

That shouldn't have touched her own anger, shouldn't have made it waver for even a second. But it did. Not that she was going to do anything about it. He was a liar, and even though that nagging pity for him still wound through her anger she ignored it.

'That's too bad.' And then, because she couldn't help herself, 'Feel free to try and change my mind if you can. But you won't be able to.'

The flame in his eyes blazed and he pushed himself away from the window, straightening to his full height. A wild thrill shot straight down her spine. Oh, yes, challenge accepted.

'You shouldn't say things like that to men like me,' he murmured. 'But, fine, you'll have your money. You'll have to come to San Lorenzo with me if you want it, though. We'll be married in my family chapel.'

Leonie didn't think twice. She wanted the money—what did she care if she had to return to Spain to get it?

Are you sure it's a good idea to be near him?

Why wouldn't it be? She didn't care about him—not now. She didn't care about her father, either. Now all she cared about was the money, and she had no problem with using Cristiano the way he'd used her.

'Fine,' she said, shrugging. 'I don't care.'

'Good.' He moved, striding past her to the door of his bedroom without even a glance. 'Prepare to leave in an hour.'

And then he went out.

CHAPTER EIGHT

CRISTIANO FILLED THE flight to Spain with business. It was the only way to distract himself from the fact that Leonie was right there, sitting casually in one of his jet's luxurious leather seats, leafing through a magazine as if the night before and the morning after had all been just a passing encounter for her.

It was a performance worthy of himself.

It also drove him mad enough that he stayed on the phone even as the car they'd transferred to from the small airport where they'd landed wound its way through the sharp crags of the mountains on the road to San Lorenzo.

He could think of no other way to handle having her in his vicinity and not touching her.

Since she had no other clothes, she wore the black T-shirt and black trousers of his staff uniform, the small bag at her side containing only her old clothes and her useless phone—items she'd insisted on bringing with her for no reason that he could see.

He hadn't argued. She could bring them if she wanted to. He was planning on providing her with a proper wardrobe anyway, once they'd got to his estate, since if she was going to be his duchess he would need her to look the part.

But even that plain black uniform didn't stop memories of the night before rolling through him. Of her silken skin beneath his fingers, of the cries she'd made, of how tightly she'd gripped him as he'd slid inside her, of the look in her eyes as she'd stared up at him.

He'd told himself that the sex didn't matter, that it was physical, nothing more, and yet he couldn't get it out of his head. Couldn't get the memory of her white face as he'd told her the truth that he'd known who she was all this time out of his head, either.

He'd been right. Not only had he shocked her, he'd hurt her, too. She hadn't even known that her father thought she was dead. And what had been worse was the feeling that had swept through him as those big violet eyes had stared back at him in shock and betrayal. The need to go to the bed and sweep her into his arms had been strong. To hold her. Soothe her. Comfort her.

But he hadn't allowed himself to give in to those feelings. Instead he'd watched as his little *gatita* had drawn on some hidden core of strength, her pain and shock vanishing beneath her usual stubborn bellig- erence and an emotion he was all too familiar with.

Anger.

He'd hoped telling her the truth would make her aware of what kind of man he was and put some distance between them, and it had. He just hadn't expected to feel quite so disappointed about that— or disappointed in her demands. The money wasn't important—it wasn't an outrageous sum—it was the fact that she didn't want him to touch her again that he cared about. Which was especially enraging since he wasn't supposed to care.

Your emotions are involved with her whether you like it or not.

Yes, which meant he had to *un*-involve them.

Difficult when touching her was all he wanted to do.

The car wound through yet another green valley, with vineyards spread out on either side, almost to the foothills of the sharp, jagged mountains rising above them. But Cristiano wasn't watching the homeland he hadn't been to in years unroll before him. He was too busy watching the woman sitting beside him.

She had her head turned away, and was staring at the view outside. The sun was falling over the fine grain of her skin and turning her hair to fire.

Beautiful *gatita*.

He couldn't stop the sound of her voice replaying in his head, even huskier than it normally was, telling him how her mother had told her that her father hadn't wanted her, that he'd wanted a son instead.

Cristiano didn't know what to think about that, because it was certainly something that Victor de Riero had wanted. And maybe it had been true that Hélène couldn't have any more children. Maybe that had been part of the reason for de Riero targeting Anna. He'd wanted a new, more fertile wife for an heir.

'*I thought he didn't look for me because he didn't care...*'

A deep sympathy he didn't want to feel sat in his chest like a boulder, weighing him down. All those years she'd been on the streets, thinking herself unwanted. Where had Hélène been? Gone, it was clear, leaving Leonie to fend for herself. Alone.

He knew that feeling. He knew what it was to be alone. He'd had it all his childhood, as the only child of a man who'd cared more about his duties as duke than being a father, and a woman who'd preferred socialite parties to being a mother.

No wonder you scared Anna away. You were an endless well of need.

Cristiano dragged his gaze from Leonie and tried to concentrate on his phone call instead of the snide voice in his head.

Another reason not to care—as if he needed one. His emotions were destructive, and he had to make sure he stayed detached from them, which meant caring about Leonie wasn't something he should do.

He shouldn't give in to this sexual hunger, either, no matter how badly he wanted to. Letting one little kitten get the better of him just wasn't going to happen.

He leaned back in his seat, shifting slightly, uncomfortable with being so long in the car. Then he noticed that Leonie had tensed. Her gaze was flicking from the window to him, her hand lifting an inch from her thigh before coming down again. Colour crept into her cheeks as she turned towards the window again.

Interesting. So she was physically aware of him, perhaps as painfully as he was aware of her, which made sense. Because she'd loved everything he'd done to her and had answered his passion with her own fierce, untutored desire. A hunger like that, once released, didn't die. It burned for ever. She wouldn't be able to ignore it the way she had on the streets.

Cristiano didn't smile, but he allowed himself a certain satisfaction, filing away her response for future reference. Then he focused completely on his phone call as the car wound its way through another vineyard and then the tiny ancient village that had once been part of his estate. They moved on up into the mountains, and from there down a rocky, twisting driveway that led at last to the *castillo* he'd been born in.

The *castillo* he'd grown up in.

The big, empty *castillo* that had echoed with nothing but silence after his parents had been killed.

And that was your fault, too.

Cristiano tensed as the car cleared the trees and Leonie sat forward as the *castillo* came into view.

'You live here?' she asked, in tones of absolute astonishment. 'In a castle?'

It was literally a castle, built into the hillside. A medieval fortress that his warlord ancestors had held for centuries. Had it really been fifteen years since he'd been back?

After Anna had gone, and he'd lost his son, it had felt too big and too empty. It had reminded him of being seventeen once again, of losing his parents and walking the halls, feeling as if the silence and the guilt was pressing in on him. Crushing him.

After Anna, he hadn't been able to get out of the place fast enough, filling up his life with music and talk and laughter. With the sound of life.

A cold sensation sat in his gut as the car drew up on the gravel area outside the massive front doors. Why had he thought coming back was a good idea? He didn't want to go inside. The whole place had felt like a tomb the last time he'd been here and nothing would have changed.

Something's changed. You have Leonie.

She was already getting out of the car, walking towards the doors, looking up in open amazement at the *castillo* towering above her.

Ah, but he didn't have her, did he? She wasn't his. She'd made that very clear.

Still, if he was going to make her his duchess he wanted it to happen on Velazquez ground, and he'd already sent messages to his PR company to let them know he'd be bringing his 'fiancée' back to his estate, and that more information would follow. They were naturally thrilled that the duke of San Lorenzo, infamous for his pursuit of pleasure, would be marrying again. The press would be ecstatic.

Gathering himself, Cristiano got out of the car and strolled after Leonie, letting none of his unease show. He'd called his staff here before he'd left Paris, telling them to prepare for his arrival, so everything should be in place.

Sure enough, they were greeted in the huge, vaulted stone entrance hall by one of his family's old retainers. The woman spoke a very old Spanish dialect that no one spoke outside the valley, and the memories it evoked made the cold inside him deepen.

He answered her in the same language, issuing orders while Leonie wandered around, looking up at the bare stone walls and the huge stone staircase that led to the upper levels. Portraits of his ancestors had been hung there. He'd always hated them—dark, gloomy paintings of stone-faced men and women who looked as if they'd never tasted joy in their entire lives and perhaps hadn't.

Leonie had started climbing the stairs to look at them and he walked slowly after her, the familiar cold oppressiveness of the ancient stones wrapping around him, squeezing him tight.

'Are these people your family?' she asked, staring at the portraits.

'Yes. Miserable bunch, aren't they?'

'They don't look that happy, no.' She frowned. 'But…they're so old. How long has your family been here?'

He climbed up a little way, then stopped one step below her, looking at her since that was better than looking at those ghastly portraits. She was all pale skin, bright hair and deep blue-violet eyes. Life and colour. Unlike these dim, dark portraits of people long dead.

'Centuries.' He thrust his hands in his pockets, his fingers itching to touch her. 'Since medieval times, if not before.'

'Wow…' she breathed, following the line of portraits on the walls. 'And what about this one?'

She pointed at the last picture, the most recent—though it didn't look like it, given it had been painted in the same dark, gloomy style. Her earlier anger at him seemed to have faded away, and interest was alight in her face.

Cristiano didn't look at the picture. He knew exactly which one it was. 'That one? Those are my parents. They were killed in a car accident when I was seventeen.'

She flicked him a glance, a crease between her brows. 'Oh. I'm sorry.'

It sounded almost as if she really meant it—not that he needed her sympathy. It had happened so long ago he barely remembered it.

That's why you can never escape the cold of this place. That's why you carry it around with you wherever you go. Because you can't remember how you tried to warm it up…

Cristiano shoved the thoughts away. 'It was a long time ago.'

'Your mother was pretty.' She leaned closer,

studying the picture. 'Your father was handsome, too. But he looks a little…stern.'

'If by "stern" you mean aloof and cold, then, yes. He was. And my mother was far more interested in parties than anything else.' He was conscious that he hadn't quite managed to hide the bitter note in his voice.

Leonie straightened and turned, studying his face. 'They weren't good parents?'

He didn't want to talk about this. 'What happened to Hélène, Leonie?' he asked instead. 'What happened to your mother?'

Her lashes fluttered; her gaze slid away. 'She left. I was sixteen. I came home from school one day and she was just…gone. She left me a note, saying she was leaving and not to look for her. But that was it.'

His fingers had curled into fists in his pockets, and that same tight sensation that Leonie always seemed to prompt was coiling in his chest. 'She just left? Without saying why?'

'Yes.' Leonie was looking down at the stairs now. 'I'll never know why.'

So. She'd effectively been abandoned by the one person in the world who should have looked after her. At sixteen.

'What did you do?' he asked quietly.

She lifted a shoulder. 'Eventually I was evicted from our apartment. No one seemed to notice I was gone.'

He felt as if a fist was closing around his ribs and

squeezing, and he wanted to reach out, touch that petal-soft cheek. Tell her that he would have noticed. That he would have looked for her.

But then she glanced up at him again, a fierce expression in her eyes. 'Don't you dare pity me. I survived on my own quite well, thank you very much.'

'Survived, maybe,' he said. 'But life isn't just survival, Leonie.'

'It's better than being dead.'

Proud, stubborn girl.

'You should have had more than that.' This time it was his turn to study her. 'You deserved more than that.'

Colour flooded her pale cheeks, shock flickering in her eyes. 'Yes, well, I didn't get it. And you didn't answer my question.'

'No,' he said. 'Mine were not good parents.'

She blinked, as if she hadn't expected him to capitulate so quickly. 'Oh. Do you have brothers or sisters?'

'No.'

'So it was just you? All alone in this big castle by yourself?' There was a certain knowledge in her eyes, an understanding that he'd never thought he'd find in anyone else.

She knew loneliness—of course she did.

'Yes.' He lifted a shoulder. 'I was alone in this big castle by myself. This mausoleum was my inheritance.'

'Is that what it felt like? A mausoleum?'

'Don't you feel it?' He moved his gaze around the soaring ceilings and bare stone walls. 'All that cold stone and nothing but dead faces everywhere. I never come here if I can help it. In fact, I haven't been here in fifteen years.'

There was silence, but he could feel her looking at him, studying him like an archaeologist studying a dig site, excavating him.

'What happened here, Cristiano?'

That was his *gatita*. Always so curious and always so blunt.

'Do I really have to go into my long and tedious history?' he drawled. 'Don't you want to see where you're going to be sleeping?'

'No. And isn't your tedious history something I should know? Especially if I'm going to be marrying you.'

He looked at her. She was so small; she was on the stair above him but she was still only barely level with him. He didn't want to talk about this any more. He wanted his hands on her instead. He wanted her warmth melting away the relentless cold of this damn tomb.

'What is there to say?'

He kept his gaze on her, hiding nothing. Because she was right. She should know his history. So she knew what to be wary of.

'It was my seventeenth birthday, but my parents had some government party they had to attend. I was lonely. I was angry. And it was the second birthday in a row that they'd missed. So I took a match to my father's library and set it on fire.'

Leonie's gaze widened. 'What?'

'You think that's the worst part? It's not.' He smiled, but it was bitter. 'One of my father's staff called him to let him know the *castillo* was on fire. So he and my mother rushed back from the party. But he drove too fast and there was an accident. They were both killed.'

She hadn't understood until that moment why he so obviously hated this place, with its ancient stones and the deep silence of history. She'd thought it was wonderful—a fortress that no one could get into. A place of security and safety. She'd never been anywhere so fascinating and she wanted to explore it from top to bottom.

But it was clear that Cristiano did not feel the same. It was obvious in every line of him.

This man had used her, hurt her, and no matter that he'd said their night together had been because he'd wanted her, she couldn't forget her anger at him and what he'd done.

Yet that didn't stop the pulse of shock that went through her, or the wave of sympathy that followed hard on its heels.

There was self-loathing in his voice, a bitterness he couldn't hide, and she knew what that meant: he blamed himself for his parents' death.

No wonder he hated this place. No wonder he thought it was a tomb. For him, it was.

'You blame yourself,' she said. 'Don't you?'

He gave another of those bitter laughs. 'Of course I blame myself. Who else is there? No one else started a fire because he couldn't handle his anger.'

Her heart tightened. Although their stations in life were so far removed from each other that the gulf between them might have been the distance from the earth to the sun, they were in fact far closer than she'd realised.

He'd lost people the same as she had.

'For years after Mamá left I blamed myself,' she said. 'I thought that maybe it was something I'd done that had made her leave. Perhaps I'd asked too many questions, disobeyed her too many times. Nagged her for something once too often.' Her throat closed unexpectedly, but she forced herself to go on. 'Or... been a girl instead of a boy.'

The bitter twist to his mouth vanished. 'Leonie—' he began.

But she shook her head. 'No, I haven't finished. What I'm trying to say is that in the end I didn't know why she'd left. I'll never know, probably. And I could have chosen to let myself get all eaten up about what I did or didn't do, or I could accept that it was her choice to leave.' Leonie stared at him. 'She didn't have to leave. I didn't make her. She choose that. Just like your father chose to return here.'

Cristiano's expression hardened. 'Of course he had to return. His son had just set fire to the—'

'No, he didn't,' she interrupted. 'He could have got a staff member to handle it. He could have decided he wasn't fit to drive and had your mother drive instead. He could have called you. But he didn't do any of those things. He chose to drive himself.'

Cristiano said nothing. He was standing on the step below her but still he was taller than she was, all broad shoulders and hard muscle encased in the dark grey wool of his suit. He wasn't wearing a tie, and the neck of his black shirt was open, exposing the smooth olive skin of his throat and the steady pulse that beat there.

She didn't know why she wanted to help him so badly—not after he'd hurt her the way he had. But she couldn't help it. She knew loneliness and grief, and she knew anger, too, and so much of what had happened to him had also happened to her.

'You are very wise, *gatita*,' he said at last, roughly. 'Where did you learn such wisdom?'

'There's not much to do on the streets but think.'

'In between all the surviving you had to do?' A thread of faint, wry amusement wound through his beautiful voice.

You deserved more than that...

A shiver chased over her skin. He'd said it as if he meant it, as if he truly believed that she had. But why would she trust what he said about anything?

'Yes,' she said blankly, her gaze caught and drawn

relentlessly to the pulse at the base of his throat once again. 'In between all that.'

She'd put her mouth over that pulse the night before. She'd tasted his skin and the beat of his heart, had run her hands over all that hard muscle and raw male power.

A throb of hunger went through her.

She'd spent most of the day trying to ignore his physical presence. She'd thought it would be easy enough to do since he'd ignored her, spending all his time on the phone. She'd been fascinated by all the new sights and sounds as they'd left Paris and flown to Spain, so that had made it easier.

But despite that—despite how she should have been concentrating on her return to her long-forgotten homeland—all she'd been conscious of was him. Of his deep, authoritative voice on the plane as he'd talked on his phone. Of his hard-muscled thigh next to hers in the car. Of the spice of his aftershave and the heat in his long, powerful body.

And she'd realised that she might ignore him all she liked, but that didn't change her hunger for him, or her innate female awareness of him as a man. It couldn't be switched off. It pulsed inside her like a giant heartbeat, making her horribly conscious that her declaration of how she wasn't going to let him touch her again had maybe been a little shortsighted.

That was another thing she hadn't understood before, yet did now. Sexual hunger hadn't ever affected her, so she'd imagined that refusing him would be easy. But it wasn't, and she felt it acutely now as he stood there staring at her, his jungle-green eyes holding her captive. As if he knew exactly what she was thinking.

Her heartbeat accelerated, the ache of desire pulsed between her thighs, and she knew her awareness of him was expanding, deepening.

He wasn't just a powerful and physically attractive man. He was also a man who seemed not to care about very much at all on the surface, yet who burned on the inside with a terrible all-consuming rage. And a rage like that only came from deep caring, from a man with a wounded heart who'd suffered a terrible loss.

At least after the deaths of his parents he'd been able to grieve. But how could he grieve a child who wasn't dead? Who was still alive and who had no idea that Cristiano was his father?

He hasn't grieved. Why do you think he's so angry?

'You'd better stop looking at me that way, *gatita*,' he murmured. 'You'll be giving me ideas.'

She ignored that, feeling her own heart suddenly painful in her chest. 'I'm sorry about your parents,' she said. But she wanted him to know that although his son might not be aware of Cristiano, she was. And that she acknowledged what the loss had meant for him. 'And I'm so sorry about your son.'

A raw emerald light flared in the duke's eyes. That wry amusement dropped away, his whole posture tightening. 'Do not speak of it.' His voice vibrated with some intense, suppressed emotion.

She didn't want to cause him pain, yet all of a sudden she wanted him to know that she understood. That she felt for him. And that to a certain extent she shared his loss—because she, too, had lost people she'd once felt something for: her mother and her father.

So she lifted a hand, thinking to reach out and touch him, having nothing else to give him but that.

'No, Leonie,' he ordered.

The word was heavy and final, freezing her in place.

'I have respected your wishes by not touching you, but don't think for one moment that it doesn't go both ways. Not when all I can think about is having you on these stairs right now, right here.'

Her heart thudded even louder. He had respected her wishes. He hadn't made one move towards her. And she... Well, she'd never thought that even though he'd broken her fledgling trust she'd still want him—and quite desperately.

So have him. It doesn't have to mean anything.

It didn't. And now there were no secrets between them, no trust to break, it could be just sex, nothing more. After all, she'd been denied so many good things—why should she deny herself this?

He'd told her she deserved better and he was certainly better than anything she'd ever had. So why couldn't she have him?

She lifted her hand and, holding his gaze, very

deliberately placed her fingertips against the line of his hard jaw, feeling the prickle of hair and the warm silk of his skin.

'Then take me,' she said softly.

He was completely still for long moments, unmoving beneath her hand. But his eyes burned with raw green fire.

'Once you change your mind there will be no coming back from it, do you understand me?' His voice was so deep, so rough. The growl of a beast. 'This is the place of my ancestors, and if I have you here that makes you mine.'

He was always trying to warn her, to frighten her. Letting her see the fire burning in the heart of the man he was beneath the veneer of a bored playboy. But Leonie had never been easily frightened. And the man behind that veneer, with his anger, his passion and his pain, was far more fascinating to her than the playboy ever had been.

She wanted that man. And she wasn't frightened of him. After all, she'd always wanted to be someone's. She might as well be his.

'Then I'll be yours,' she said simply.

Cristiano didn't hesitate. Reaching out, he curled his fingers around the back of her neck and pulled her in close, his mouth taking hers in a kiss that scoured all thought from her head. He kissed her hungrily, feverishly, his tongue pushing deep into her mouth and taking charge of her utterly.

But his wasn't the only hunger.

Desire leapt inside her and she put her hands on his chest, sliding them up and around his neck, threading her fingers in the thick black silk of his hair and holding on tight. She kissed him back the way she had the night before, as hard and demanding as he was, showing him her teeth and her claws by biting him.

He growled deep in his throat. His hands were on her hips, pushing her down onto the cold stone of the stairs so she was sitting on one step while he knelt on the one below her.

He didn't speak, making short work of the fastenings of her trousers and then stripping them off her, taking her underwear with them. The stone was icy under her bare skin, but she didn't care. She was burning up. Everywhere he touched felt as if it was being licked by flame.

His mouth ravaged hers, nipping and biting at her bottom lip before moving down her neck to taste the hollow of her throat. She sighed, her head falling back as he cradled the back of it in his palm. His hand slid between her bare thighs, stroking and teasing, finding her slick and hot for him.

Leonie moaned, desperate for more pressure, more friction. Desperate for more of him.

And it seemed he felt the same, because there were no niceties today, no slow, gentle seduction. He ripped open the front of his trousers, his hands falling away from her as he grabbed for his wallet and dealt with the issue of protection. Then his hot palms were sliding beneath her buttocks, lifting her, positioning her, before he pushed into her in a hard, deep thrust.

The edge of the stair above her was digging into her back. She didn't care, though, was barely conscious of it as she gasped aloud, staring up into his face. Again, he was nothing but a predator, his eyes glittering with desire, his sensual mouth drawn into a snarl as he drew his hips back and thrust again.

All she could see was that hot stare and the possessive fire in it, and it twisted the pleasure tighter, harder. She wanted to be possessed. She wanted to be taken. And she wanted to take in return. Because, as much as he wanted her to be his, she wanted something to call her own.

He could be that for you.

Her heart slammed against her ribs and she curled her legs around his lean waist, holding him tightly to her, forgetting how he'd hurt her, how he'd lied to her in that moment.

'You could be mine, too,' she whispered hoarsely as he thrust into her again, making her gasp in pleasure. 'You could be, Cristiano.'

He didn't reply, but the fire in his eyes climbed higher. His fingers curled into her hair, protecting her head from the hard stone of the stairs, but he gave her no mercy from the brutal thrust of his hips. As if he could impress himself into her. As if he was trying to make her part of the stones of the castle itself.

And beneath the passion she could feel his need,

could sense it in some deep part of her heart. The need for touch and warmth and connection. So she gave it to him, wrapping herself around him, and he took it, holding tight to her as he gave her the most intense pleasure in return.

It didn't take long.

He grabbed one her hands and guided her own fingers between her thighs, holding it down over that tight, aching bundle of nerves. And then he thrust again, deeper, harder, as he held her fingers there until the desperation inside her exploded into ecstasy and the entrance hall rang with the sounds of her cries.

She was hardly aware of his own growl as he followed her, murmuring her name roughly against her neck.

For long moments afterwards she didn't want to move, quite happy to sit on the cold stone of the stairs, with Cristiano's heat warming her through. But then he was shifting, withdrawing from her, dealing with the aftermath. Only after that was done did he reach for her, gathering her up into his arms and holding her close against his chest as he climbed the rest of the way up the stairs.

He carried her down a long and echoing stone corridor and into a room with a massive four-poster bed pushed against one wall. There he stripped her naked, put her down on it, and proceeded to make her forget her own name.

CHAPTER NINE

CRISTIANO FINISHED UP the phone call he was on with his PR people then leaned back in the old hand-carved wooden chair that sat behind his father's massive antique desk, reflecting once again on how hideously uncomfortable it was.

His father had liked the chair—his father had liked all the heavy old wooden furniture in the ducal study—but Cristiano had already decided that the chair had to go. Especially if he was going to make his home here—and he was certainly considering it.

The *castillo* was different with Leonie in it. She'd spent the past week investigating every corner of the ancient stones, exclaiming over things like the deep window seat in the library that could be enclosed when the heavy velvet curtains were drawn. Like the big bathroom that had been modernised to a point, but still retained a giant round bath of beaten copper. The cavernous dining room, where he'd had many a silent dinner with his parents, now filled up with Leonie's questions about the history of the estate and the *castillo* itself. Like the tapestries on the walls and the huge kitchen fireplace that was large enough to roast a whole cow in and probably had. The courtyard with the overgrown rose garden, the orchard full of orange trees, and the meadow beyond where he'd used to play as a child, pretending he had brothers and sisters to play with him.

But those memories seemed distant now—especially now he'd created new ones. Memories that were all about her laughter, her husky voice, her bright smile. Her cries of pleasure. Her bright hair tangled in his fingers and her warmth as he took her in yet another of those old, cold rooms.

He'd even taken her in that window seat in the library, and the memories of books flaming and shelves burning as bright as his anger were buried under flames and heat of a different kind.

It was better—much better. And the castle didn't feel so cold any more, or so silent. In fact, it felt as if summer had come to stay in the halls, making the place seem warmer and so much brighter than he remembered.

He was even considering staying on here with her after the wedding—and why not? She would be his wife, after all, and now they were spending every night, not to mention quite a few days, exploring the chemistry between them, it seemed only logical to indulge in a honeymoon, as it were. Maybe even beyond that.

He'd thought about the possibility of having an heir with her and tainting that precious de Riero bloodline even before they'd left Paris, and the idea certainly still held its appeal. He could create a home here with her. Create a family the way Victor de Riero had created a family.

You really want to have another child?

Something jolted inside him, a kind of electric shock, and he had to push himself out of his chair and take a couple of steps as restlessness coiled tight through his muscles.

Another child...

Intellectually, the idea was a sound one, and it would certainly make his revenge all the sweeter—so why did the thought make him feel as if ice was gathering in the pit of his stomach?

'I'm so sorry about your son...'

The memory of Leonie's voice on the stairs drifted back to him, the sound husky with emotion, her eyes full of a terrible sympathy, bringing with it another hard, electric jolt.

It had felt as if she was cutting him open that day, and he'd told her not to speak of it before he'd been able to stop himself. Before he'd been able to pretend that the thought of his child no longer had the power to hurt him.

So much for detachment.

His hands dropped into fists at his sides and he took a slow breath.

Yes, he could recognise that the thought of having another child was difficult for him, but he also had to recognise that this situation was different.

Any child he had with Leonie would be born in pursuit of his revenge, nothing more. It would not be for him. Which meant it was perfectly possible for him to remain detached.

He would simply choose not to involve himself with any such child, and that would be better for the child, too. Certainly he wouldn't love it—not when love led to nothing but pain and destruction. The cost of love had been too high the first time; he wouldn't pay it again.

At that moment the heavy wooden door of the study burst open and he turned to find Leonie sweeping in, a blur of shimmering white silk and silvery lace, her hair in a loose, bright cascade down her back. She came to a stop in front of him, her cornflower-blue eyes alight with excitement, and put her hands on her hips.

'Well?' she asked. 'What do you think of this?'

He stared, all thoughts of children vanishing, his chest gone tight.

She was wearing a wedding gown. It was strapless, the gleaming white silk bodice embroidered with silver and cupping her breasts deliciously. Then it narrowed down to her small waist before sweeping outwards in a white froth of silky skirts and silver lace.

She looked beautiful—a princess from a fairytale or a queen about to be crowned.

'You forgot, didn't you?' she said as he stared at

her in stunned silence. 'The designer's here with a few of the dresses we picked last week.'

He *had* forgotten. He and Leonie had sat down the previous week to choose a gown for her—not that he'd been overly interested in the details of the wedding, since it was the revenge that mattered. But Leonie had been excited, and had enjoyed choosing a gown for herself, and he'd surprised himself by enjoying helping her, too.

'So I see.' He tried to calm his racing heartbeat, unable to take his eyes off her. 'I'm not supposed to see the final gown before the wedding, am I?'

'Well, it's your revenge. I thought you might want to make sure the dress is...' she did a small twirl, the gown flaring out around her '...revengey enough.'

Her excitement and pleasure were a joy, and yet they only added to that tight sensation in his chest— the one he hadn't asked for and didn't want, and yet had been there since the night he'd picked her up off the street.

He fought it, tried to ignore it. 'You like it, don't you?'

She smiled, her expression radiant, her hands smoothing lovingly over the silk. 'I love it. I've never had anything so pretty or that's felt so lovely.'

She'd been like this over the past couple of weeks as he'd bought clothes and other personal items to add to her meagre stock of belongings, greeting each new thing with a thrilled delight that was immensely gratifying. And it didn't matter whether it was expensive or not—the fact that she had something of her own seemed to be the most important thing.

It made sense. She'd literally had nothing when he'd found her that night on the streets of Paris except for a very old cellphone and some dirty clothes. Now she had a wardrobe full of items she'd chosen with great care herself and a new phone, not to mention shoes and underwear and perfume and lots of other pretty girly things.

But he hadn't felt like this when he'd given her those things and she'd smiled at him. Not like he did now, with her so radiantly lovely in a wedding gown, full of excitement and joy. He hadn't felt as if he couldn't breathe…as if the world was tilting on its axis and he was going to slide right off.

All he could think about was the day they'd arrived here and how he'd told her that once he took her here, in the place of his ancestors, she'd be his. And how she'd surrendered to him as if she'd never wanted to be anyone else's, all the while whispering to him that he was hers, too.

You want to be hers.

No, he didn't. He couldn't be anyone's—just as he couldn't have anything that was his. Not any more. Not when he couldn't trust himself and his destructive emotions. And this tight feeling in his chest, the way he couldn't breathe…

You're falling for her.

Absolutely not. He had to stay detached and uninvolved. Keep it all about revenge. Because that, in the end, was the whole point of this charade: a cold and emotionless revenge against the man who'd taken his wife and son from him.

Which meant he had to keep his emotions out of it.

Yet still he couldn't stop himself from touching her, reaching out to brush his fingers over the lace of her bodice, watching as her eyes darkened with the passion that always burned so near the surface. She was always ready for him. She never denied him.

'You are beautiful, *gatita*,' he murmured. 'You are perfect in every way.'

She flushed adorably, giving him a little smile. 'Thank you.' Then that smile faded, a look of concern crossing her face. 'Are you all right?'

How she'd picked up on his unease he had no idea, because he was sure he'd hidden it. Then again, she was incredibly perceptive. Too perceptive in many ways.

'What? I can't give my fiancée a compliment without my health being questioned?' he asked, keeping his voice casual. 'Whatever is the world coming to?'

She didn't smile. 'Cristiano…'

The tight thing in his chest tightened even further, like a fist. 'You know this will be a proper marriage, don't you?' They hadn't had this conversation and they needed to. It might as well be now. 'You'll be my wife in every way?'

'Yes,' she replied without hesitation. 'You made that clear.'

'I will want children, too.'

This time her gaze flickered. 'Oh.'

'It makes my revenge even more perfect, *gatita*. Don't you see? He took my son and I will have another with his daughter.'

An expression he couldn't catch rippled over her face, then abruptly her lashes lowered, veiling her gaze. 'I do see, yes.' Her tone was utterly neutral.

He stared down at the smooth, silky curve of her cheek and the brilliant colour of her lashes resting against her pale skin. She seemed a little less bright now, her excitement dimming, disappearing.

'You don't like the idea of children?' he asked.

'No. I just…just hadn't thought of them before.'

He couldn't blame her. She was young, and probably hadn't considered a future with a family. But still, he didn't think it was surprise she was trying to hide from him—and she was definitely hiding something.

Reaching out, he took her chin between his thumb and forefinger and tilted her face up so he could look into her eyes. 'This bothers you. Why?'

She made no attempt to pull away, her violet gaze meeting his. 'You'd really want another child? After what happened with your son?'

Ah, she never shied away from the difficult questions, did she?

'It will be different this time.' He stroked her chin gently with his thumb, unable to resist the feel of her satiny skin. 'Because the child won't be for me. The child will be for the pleasure of seeing Victor de Riero's face when I tell him he will have a Velazquez grandchild.'

That way he could retain his distance. He'd never have to feel what he'd felt for his son for another child again. Never have to experience the pain of another loss. Anger was the only emotion he could allow himself to have.

Some expression he couldn't name shifted in her eyes. 'That's a terrible reason to have a child, Cristiano.'

The flat note of accusation in her voice burrowed like a knife between his ribs, making him realise how cold and callous he'd sounded.

He let go of her chin, felt the warmth of her skin lingering against his fingertips. 'Too bad. That's the only reason I'll ever have another.'

Cold and callous it would have to be. He couldn't afford anything else.

'Revenge…' The word echoed strangely off the stone walls of the room, her gaze never leaving his. 'Don't you want more than that?'

Something inside him dropped away, while something else seemed to claw its way up. Longing. The same kind of longing that had gripped him the day he'd taken her on the staircase of this *castillo*. The need for her touch, for the feel of her skin and the taste of her mouth. The heat of her body burning out the cold.

The need for *her*.

He couldn't allow that. Need had caused him more pain than anything else ever had, so he'd cut it out of his life. Successfully. He had no desire to let it back in again.

'No.' He kept his voice cold. 'I don't.'

But she only looked at him in that direct, sharp way. Seeing beneath the armour of the playboy duke that he wore, seeing the man beneath it. The desperate, lonely man…

'Yes, you do,' she said quietly. 'Would it really be so bad? To let yourself have more?'

Ah, his *gatita*. She couldn't leave well enough alone, could she? She should really learn when to stop pushing.

'I had more once,' he said. 'And I lost it. I do not want it again.'

Those big violet eyes searched his. 'Because of your son? Because of Anna?'

He should have laughed. Should have lifted a shoulder and made a joke. Should have closed the distance between them and put his hands on her, distracted her the way he knew so well how to do.

But he didn't do any of those things. He turned away from her instead and moved around his desk. 'I told you before—do not speak of them. They have nothing to do with our wedding.'

He sat down in his father's uncomfortable chair, ignoring the way his heart was beating, ignoring the pain that had settled in his heart for absolutely no reason that he could see.

'Now, if there's nothing else, I have some work to do.'

Except Leonie didn't move. She just stood there in the lovely gown, looking at him. Sympathy in her eyes. 'It wasn't your fault, Cristiano. What happened with my father and Anna…with your son.'

The knife between his ribs sank deeper, pain rippling outwards, and he found he was gripping the arms of the chair so hard his knuckles were white. 'I told you. Do not—'

'You were young and you didn't know.' Leonie was suddenly standing right in front of his desk, that terrible piercing gaze of hers on him. 'You were used. You were betrayed by someone you thought you could trust.' There was blue flame burning in her eyes, conviction in her voice. 'And you had every right—*every right*—to be angry.'

'No,' he heard himself say hoarsely, and then he was on his feet, his hands in fists, fury flooding through him. 'Maybe I did have every right, but I should have controlled it. Controlled myself. I barged into that party, shouting like a monster, and I scared my son, Leonie. I *terrified* him. And he ran straight to Victor as if I was the devil himself.'

His jaw ached, his every muscle stiff with tension, and he wanted to stop talking but the words kept on coming.

'I would have taken him, too. I would have ripped him from Victor's arms if Anna hadn't stopped me. If she hadn't thrown herself in front of Victor and told me that this was why she'd left me. Because I terrified her.'

Leonie was coming, moving around the side of the desk towards him, and he shoved the chair back, wanting to put some distance between them. But she was there before he could move, reaching out to cup his face between her small hands.

'You're *not* to blame,' she insisted, her voice vibrating with fierce emotion. 'That man—my *father*—' she spat the word as if it were poison '—took your son from you. He seduced your wife from you. He had no right. And it was *not* your fault. Just like the deaths of your parents weren't your fault.'

The fire in her eyes was all-consuming, mesmerising.

'Just like it wasn't my fault my mother left and my father just accepted I was dead and never once looked for confirmation.'

Her grip held him still, her conviction almost a physical force.

'You were angry because you cared about him, Cristiano. And, yes, caring hurts—but wouldn't you rather have had the pain than feel nothing for him? Than for all of that to have meant nothing at all?'

He couldn't move. He was held in place by her hands on him. By the passion and fierce anger that burned in her lovely face. Passion that burned for *him*.

His world tilted again and he was falling right off the face of it. And there was no one to hold on to but her.

Cristiano reached for her, hauled her close. And crushed her mouth beneath his.

Leonie was shaking as Cristiano kissed her, sliding her hands down the wall of his rock-hard chest, curling her fingers into his shirt, holding on to him.

She hadn't meant to confront him. Hadn't meant to hurt him. But she knew she *had* hurt him. She'd seen the flare of agony in his green eyes as she'd mentioned his son, had heard the harsh rasp of it in his beautiful voice as he'd told her that he'd lost what he'd had. And so, no, he didn't want more.

But he'd lied. Of course he wanted more. She felt his longing every time he touched her, every time he pushed inside her. It was there in the demanding way he kissed her, in the brutal rhythm of his hips as he claimed her, stamping his possession on her. In the way he said her name when he came, and in the way he held her so tightly afterwards, as if he didn't want her to get away.

That was fine with her; she loved the way he wanted her. But she hadn't understood why he kept denying that was what he wanted until now. Until he'd tried to end the conversation.

It had all become clear to her then.

Of course he didn't want more. Because he blamed himself for the loss of his wife and child and he thought he didn't deserve more.

She'd told him that day on the stairs that he wasn't responsible for his parents' death, but it was clear that he hadn't taken that on board. That the guilt he was carrying around extended to the loss of his son.

And she didn't know why, but his pain had felt like a knife in her own heart.

She hadn't been able to stop the fierce anger that had risen inside her on his behalf, the fierce need to make him understand that he didn't have to take responsibility for what had happened because it wasn't his fault. None of it was.

He might act as if he was frightening, as if he was bad, but he wasn't. There was nothing about him that was cruel or mean or petty. That was violent or bullying. He was simply a man whose emotions ran fathoms deep and so very strong. A man who'd lost so very much.

She couldn't bear to see him hurt.

He gripped her tight, lifting her, then turning to put her on the desk, ravaging her mouth as he did so. She spread her legs, dropping her hands to his lean hips to pull him closer, the fall of her skirts getting in the way.

'Leonie,' he said hoarsely against her mouth. 'Not like this, *gatita*. Not again.'

'But I—'

He laid a finger across her mouth and she was stunned to feel it tremble lightly against her lips. His eyes had darkened, the green almost black.

'I want to savour you, *mi corazón*. I don't want to be a beast today.'

'I like the beast,' she murmured.

But that was all he gave her a chance to say, because then his mouth was on hers again, his hands moving down the bodice of the beautiful wedding gown, his fingers shaping her through the fabric, cupping her breasts gently in his palms.

She shivered, because there was something reverent in his touch that hadn't been there before. As if she was a work of art that he had to be careful in handling.

You're not a work of art. You're dirt from the streets—don't forget.

No, she didn't believe it. And she didn't feel it, either—not as his kiss turned gentle, teasing.

The passion between them that normally flared hot and intense had become more focused, more deliberate, settling on delicacy and tenderness rather than mastery.

He tasted her mouth, exploring it lightly before brushing his lips over her jaw and down the side of her neck in a trail of kisses and gentle nips that had her shuddering in his hands. He didn't speak but he didn't need to; the reverent way he touched her made it clear. He'd said he wanted to savour her and that was exactly what he was doing.

He unzipped the gown and slid it down her body, lifting her up so he could get it off her, then laying it carefully over the desk. He turned back to her and pushed her down over the polished wood, so she was lying across the desk next to her gown.

Slowly, carefully, he stripped her underwear from

her, his fingers running lightly over every curve, and with each touch she felt something inside her shift and change. She had become something else…something more. Not the dirty, unwanted girl from the streets but someone treasured. Someone precious.

His hands swept down her body, stroking, caressing, as if she was beautiful, wanted, worth taking time over. And, perhaps for the first time in her life, Leonie actually felt that. Tears prickled behind her lids, her throat was tight, but she didn't fight the sensations or the emotions that came along with them, letting them wash through her as he touched her, as if his hands were sweeping them away for good.

He kissed his way down her body, teasing her nipples with his tongue, then drawing them inside the heat of his mouth, making her arch and gasp. His hands stroked her sides and then moved further down, along her thighs. With each caress the dirt of the streets fell away, and with it the cold loneliness and the isolation.

She would have let him touch her for ever if she could, but soon her entire body was trembling and she wanted more from him than gentle touches. She sat up, pushed her hands beneath his shirt, stroking the hard, chiselled muscles of his stomach, glorying in the heat of his skin. Glorying too in the rough curse he gave as she dropped one hand to the fastenings of his trousers and undid them, slipping her hand inside, curling her fingers around his shaft.

'Ah, *gatita*…' he murmured roughly, letting her

stroke him. 'You should let me finish proving my point.'

'Which is…?' She looked up into his green eyes, losing herself in the heat that burned there. 'That you're not a beast? I know that already.'

'No. My point is that you're worth savouring.'

'Well, so are you.' She ran her fingers lightly along the length of him, loving how he shuddered under her touch. 'You're not the only one worth taking time over.'

His gaze darkened. *'Mi corazón…'*

He didn't believe her, did he?

'Here,' she said thickly. 'Let me show you.'

And she pushed at him so he shifted back, then slid off his desk to stand before him, going up on her tiptoes to kiss the strong column of his neck and then further down, tasting the powerful beat of the pulse at his throat. Then she undid the buttons of his shirt, running her fingers down his sculpted torso, tracing all those hard-cut muscles before dropping to her knees in front of him.

Her hands moved to part the fabric of his trousers, to grasp him and take out the long, hard length of him. And then she closed her mouth around him.

His hands slid into her hair and he gave a rough groan, flexing his hips. He tasted so good, a little salty and musky, and she loved the way she could make his breath catch and his body shake. But she also loved giving him pleasure—because if she deserved to feel wanted and treasured, then he did, too.

So she showed him, worshipping him with her mouth until he finally pulled her head away, picking her up in his arms and taking her over to the butter-soft leather couch under the window. He laid her down on it, dealt with protection, then spread her thighs, positioning himself. And when he pushed inside her it felt like a homecoming, a welcome rather than something desperate and hungry.

He didn't move at first, and she lost herself in the green of his eyes and the feel of him inside her, filling her. There was a rightness to this. A sense of wholeness. As if she'd been waiting for this moment, for him, her entire life.

You're in love with him.

Something shifted in her chest, a heavy weight, and it made her go hot and cold both at the same time. Made her dizzy and hungry, bursting with happiness and aching with despair all at once.

Was what she felt love? How would she know? No one had ever given her love. She'd never even contemplated it before.

Yet the hot, powerful thing inside her, pushing at her, was insistent, and she had no other name for it. And it was all centred on him. On his beautiful face and the heat in his eyes. On his smile and the dark, sexy sound of his laughter. On the way he touched her, the way he made her feel. As if she wasn't broken or dirty, but beautiful and full of light. A treasure, precious and wanted.

He began to move inside her and she couldn't

look away. The feeling suffusing her entire body was making her ache. She'd never known till that moment that pain could have a sweet edge.

Words stuck in her throat. Part of her wanted to tell him. Yet something held her back.

'I had more. And I lost it.'

And she was simply a replacement for what he'd lost, wasn't she? A handy vehicle for his revenge. He pitied her and wanted her, that was clear, but that was all she was to him.

Why don't you just ask him?

But she didn't want to ask him. She would lose this moment, and the moment was all she'd ever had. The moment was all there was.

So she ignored the heavy feeling in her heart, in her soul, and pulled his mouth down on hers. Losing herself to his heat and his kiss and the pleasure he could give her and letting the future take care of itself.

CHAPTER TEN

CRISTIANO WAITED IN a small side room in the ancient chapel that had once been part of the Velazquez estate. Many of his ancestors had been christened and married in this same place, before making their final journey from there to the small cemetery at the back.

He'd waited for a bride here before, his heart beating fast with happiness and excitement as he'd watched through the window for her arrival.

Today, although he was waiting for another bride, it wasn't her he was watching for, and he felt neither excitement nor happiness. He felt cold, and a bone-deep anger was the only thing warming him as he watched for de Riero.

Initially there had been some doubt as to whether the man would accept the invitation, but curiosity and perhaps a chance to gloat had clearly won out, because he'd passed on his acceptance to one of Cristiano's staff.

Guests were already streaming in, and journalists were gathering as per his instructions to his PR people. He wanted as many news media people there as possible to record the moment when he would lift Leonie's veil and reveal her for the first time. To record Victor's face when he realised that it was his daughter standing at the altar.

The daughter who was supposed to be dead.

The daughter who was now his hated enemy's bride.

The daughter who doesn't deserve this pettiness.

Cristiano gritted his teeth, shifting restlessly as he watched the guests enter the chapel.

It wasn't pettiness. It was necessary. How else was he to deal with losing everything that had ever meant something to him?

Doesn't she also mean something to you?

The memory of Leonie's touch wound through him. Not her mouth on him, but her hands cupping his face. That fierce, passionate gaze staring up into his, telling him that none of it was his fault. As if it was vitally important to her that he understand that. As if *he* was important to her.

His hands closed into fists as he gazed sightlessly through the window.

No, he couldn't think about this—about her. It was vital his emotions stay out of it. The important thing was that he was very close to finally getting the satisfaction he craved from de Riero—payback for the agony he had caused him—and nothing was going to stop him from getting it.

And after that?

Cristiano ignored the thought, focusing instead

on the long black car that now drew up in the gravel parking area outside the chapel and the tall man that got out of it.

De Riero.

Cristiano began to smile.

And then de Riero turned as another person got out of the car. A tall, gangly teenager with a shock of black hair. De Riero said something and the boy straightened up, looking sullen. Then he reached to adjust the boy's tie, and he must have said something else because the boy lost his sullen look, grinning reluctantly.

An arrow of pure agony pierced Cristian's heart.

His son.

He couldn't move, couldn't tear his gaze away. He purposely hadn't looked at any pictures of the boy, or read any news stories about him. He'd simply pretended that the child had never existed.

But he did exist. And now he was here. And he was tall, handsome. He'd grow into those shoulders one day, just as he'd grow into his confidence, and then the world would be his oyster. He'd be a credit to his parents…

But Cristiano would not be one of those parents.

Pain spread outwards inside him, a grief he wasn't prepared for. Why had de Riero brought the boy? To gloat? To rub salt in the wound? As a shield? Why?

And then another person got out of the car—a woman with dark hair in a dark blue dress. Anna.

She came to stand by her son, smiling up at him,

saying something to both him and de Riero that made them laugh. De Riero put a hand at the small of her back and leaned in to kiss her cheek while Anna's hand rested on her son's shoulder.

Something else hit Cristiano with all the force of a quarrel shot from a crossbow.

They were happy.

His son was happy.

You will destroy that. Publicly.

Realisation washed over him like a bucket of ice water and he found himself turning from the window and striding into the middle of the room, his hands in fists.

Anger was a torch blazing inside him. Of course de Riero had brought the boy. Yes, he *was* here as a shield—to protect de Riero against anything Cristiano might do. The coward. Well, he was mistaken. This wedding would go ahead, and Cristiano would parade his daughter in front of him, and...

In front of your son.

Cristiano took a breath, then another, adrenaline pumping through him, anger and bitterness gathering in his throat, choking him.

He couldn't stop thinking about it—about what would happen when Leonie was revealed. What de Riero would do and, more importantly, what his son would do. Did he know he had a stepsister? If he did, how would he react to the knowledge that she wasn't dead, but alive? And if he didn't what would he think about the fact that his so-called father hadn't told him?

That happiness you saw outside... You will destroy it. In front of the world.

The breath caught in his throat, an arrow reaching his heart.

He couldn't do it.

He couldn't destroy his son's happiness.

He'd already done it once before, when the boy had been small, frightening him and sending straight into de Riero's arms. He couldn't do it again.

And all the revenge in the world wouldn't give him back what he'd lost. That was gone. For ever.

Love. That was the problem. That had *always* been the problem.

He'd loved his parents and, no matter what Leonie said, that love had destroyed them. He'd loved Anna once, and had nearly destroyed her. And this love he had for his son—well, now he was on the brink of nearly destroying him, too.

This revenge wasn't cold. It burned like the sun and that was unacceptable.

Love. He was done with it.

And Leonie? What about her?

Yes, she was another casualty of his caring. He'd drawn her into his orbit and kept her there—a tool he could use, a weapon he could wield against Victor de Riero.

Lovely, generous, passionate Leonie, who didn't deserve the use he'd put her to.

Who deserved so much more than being tied to man who only saw her only as something he could use.

He was selfish and he'd hurt her. And he would keep on hurting her. Because that was all he knew how to do.

Hurting people was all he ever did.

Certainty settled down inside him, along with a bone-deep pain and regret. He should never have picked her up off the street and taken her home. Or at least he should have found her a place to live and a job far away from him, where she would have been able to create the kind of life she wanted, not be dragged into his own self-centred plans.

Anna was right to be afraid of you.

His hand was shaking as he grabbed his phone from his pocket and called one of his assistants to get Leonie's location. Luckily she was still a few minutes away, so he ordered the assistant to get the driver to bring the car around to the back of the chapel instead of the front. He'd get another member of staff to intercept her and bring her here, where he could talk to her, tell her what he intended to do.

He paced around for ten minutes, conscious that the moment when they were supposed to exchange vows was getting closer and closer, and that the sooner he made an announcement the better. But he needed to tell her first. She deserved that from him at least.

Finally the door opened and Leonie was ushered in.

His heart shuddered to a complete halt inside his chest.

She was in that gorgeous wedding dress, a princess out of a fairy-tale. The veil that covered her face was white lace, densely embroidered with silver thread, and all that could be seen was the faint gleam of her red-gold hair. In one hand was a spray of simple wildflowers, gathered from the meadow near the castle, while the other held her skirts out of the way so she could walk.

His beautiful *gatita*.

She will never be yours.

He hadn't thought that particular truth would hurt, but it did, like a sword running through him. He ignored the pain. He wouldn't be the cause of any more hurt for her. She'd had enough of that in her life already.

'What's happening?' Leonie pushed back her veil, revealing her lovely face, her cornflower-blue eyes wide and filling with concern as they saw his face. 'What's going on, Cristiano? Are you okay? You look like you've seen a ghost.'

The deep violet-blue of her eyes was the colour that he only ever saw on the most perfect days here in the valley. The warmth of her body was like the hot, dry summers that were his only escape from the silence and the cold. Her rich, heady scent was like the rose garden hidden in the courtyard, where he'd used to play as a child.

She was everything good. Everything he'd been searching for and never known he'd wanted.

Everything he could never have—not when he'd only end up destroying it.

He stood very still, shutting out the anger and the pain, the deep ache of regret that settled inside him. Shutting out every one of those terrible, raw, destructive emotions.

'I'm sorry, *gatita*,' he said. 'But I'm going to have to cancel the wedding.'

Leonie stared at the man she'd thought she'd be marrying today, shock rippling through her. She'd been nervous that morning as a couple of Cristiano's staff had helped her prepare for the ceremony, doing her hair and make-up, preparing her bouquet and finally helping her into the gown.

But she wasn't nervous about finally seeing her father after all these years. In fact, she'd barely thought about him, and even when she had it had only been with a savage kind of anger. Not for herself and what he'd done to her, but for what he'd done to Cristiano.

No, it was marrying Cristiano that she was nervous about. And she was nervous because she was hopelessly in love with him and had no idea what that was going to mean. Especially when she was certain he didn't feel the same about her.

She'd had a battle with herself about whether or not to tell him about her feelings and had decided in the end not to. What would telling him achieve?

Who knew how he'd take it? Perhaps things would change, and she didn't want that.

Anyway, she knew that he did feel something for her, because he showed her every night in the big four-poster bed in his bedroom. It was enough. She didn't need him to love her. She'd survived for years without love, after all, and she'd no doubt survive the rest of her life without it, too.

Of course there had been a few nagging doubts here and there. Such as how he'd mentioned having children, but said they wouldn't be for him. They'd only be in service to his grand revenge plan. That had seemed especially bleak to her, but then she couldn't force him to care if he didn't want to. She would just love any children they had twice as much, to make up for his lack.

What was important was that now she had her little cottage in the countryside—although the cottage had turned out to be a castle and she had a genuine duke at her side. She had more than enough.

More than the homeless and bedraggled Leonie of the streets had ever dreamed of.

Except now, as she stood there in her wedding gown, staring at the man she'd been going to marry, whose green eyes were bleak, she suddenly realised that perhaps all of those things hadn't been enough after all.

'What do you mean, cancel the wedding?' Her voice sounded far too small and far too fragile in the little stone room. 'I thought you were going to—?'

'I thought so, too,' he interrupted coolly. 'And then I changed my mind.'

She swallowed, trying to get her thoughts together, trying not to feel as if the ground had suddenly dropped away beneath her feet. 'Cristiano—' she began.

'De Riero has arrived,' he went on, before she could finish. 'And he has brought my son and my ex-wife with him.'

Leonie stared at him. 'You…weren't expecting them?'

'I didn't even think about them.' He was standing so still, as if he'd been turned to stone. 'Until I saw them get out of the car. And then there he was—my son. And Anna. De Riero's *family.*'

He said the word as if it hurt him, and maybe it did, because it was definitely pain turning his green eyes into shards of cut glass.

'They are happy, Leonie. My son is happy. And going through with this will hurt him. Publicly. I have no issue with doing that to de Riero, but I cannot do that to my child.' He paused a moment, staring at her. 'And I cannot do that to you, either.'

She blinked. 'What? You're not hurting me. And as for my father—'

'It won't bring my son back,' Cristiano cut her off, and the thread of pain running through his voice was like a vein of rust in a strong steel column. 'It won't make up for all the years I've missed with him. And I've already hurt him once before, years ago.

Revenge won't make me his father, but...' A muscle ticked in his strong jaw, his eyes glittering. 'Protecting him is what a father would do.'

Something twisted in her gut—sympathy, pain.

How could she argue with him? How could she put herself and what she wanted before his need to do what was right for his son?

Because that was the problem. She wanted to marry him. She wanted to be his.

'I see,' she said a little thickly. 'So what will happen? After you cancel the wedding?'

He lifted a shoulder, as if the future didn't matter. 'Everyone will go home and life will resume as normal, I expect.'

'I mean what about us, Cristiano? What will happen with us?'

But she knew as soon as the words left her mouth what the answer was. Because he'd turned away, moving over to the window, watching as the last of the guests entered the chapel.

'I think it's best if you return to Paris, Leonie,' he said quietly, confirming it. 'It's no life for you here.'

Why so surprised? He was only ever using you and you knew that.

No, she shouldn't be surprised. And it shouldn't feel as if he was cutting her heart into tiny pieces. She'd known right from the beginning what he wanted from her, and now he wasn't going to go through with his revenge plan he had no more use for her.

He'd told her she was his. But he'd lied.

Her throat closed up painfully, tears prickling in her eyes. 'No life for me? A castle in Spain isn't as good as being homeless on the streets of Paris? Is that what you're trying to say?'

He glanced at her, his gaze sharp and green and cold. 'You really think I'd turn you back out onto the streets? No, that will not happen. I'll organise a house for you, and a job, set up a weekly allowance for you to live on. You won't be destitute. You can have a new life.'

She found she was clutching her bouquet tightly. Too tightly. 'I don't want that,' she said, a sudden burst of intense fury going through her. 'I don't want *any* of those things. I'd rather sleep on the streets of Paris for ever than take whatever pathetic scraps you choose to give me!'

He looked tired all of a sudden, like a soldier who'd been fighting for days and was on his last legs. 'Then what do you want?'

She knew. She'd known for the past few weeks and hadn't said anything. Had been too afraid to ask for what she wanted in case things might change. Too afraid to reach for more in case she lost what she had.

But now he was taking that away from her she had nothing left to lose.

Leonie took a step forward, propelled by fury and a sudden, desperate longing. 'You,' she said fiercely. 'I want you.'

His face blanked. 'Me?'

And perhaps she should have stopped, should have reconsidered. Perhaps she should have stayed quiet, taken what he'd chosen to give her and created a new life for herself out of it. Because that was more than enough. More than she'd ever dreamed of.

But that had been before Cristiano had touched her, had held her, had made her feel as if she was worth something. Before he'd told her she deserved more than a dirty alleyway and a future with no hope.

Before he'd told her that she was perfect in every way there was.

'Yes, you.' She lifted her chin, held his gaze, gathering every ounce of courage she possessed. 'I love you, Cristiano. I've loved for you for weeks. And the kind of life I want is a life with you in it.'

For a second the flame in his eyes burned bright and hot, and she thought that perhaps he felt the same way she did after all. But then, just as quickly, the flame died, leaving his gaze nothing but cold green glass.

'That settles it, then,' he said, with no discernible emotion. 'You have to leave.'

She went hot, then cold, an endless well of disappointment and pain opening up inside her.

You always knew he didn't want you. Come on— why would he?

She ignored the thought, staring at him. 'Why?' she demanded.

His eyes got even colder. 'Because I don't love

you and I never will. And I have nothing else but money to give you.'

The lump in her throat felt like a boulder, the ache in her heart never-ending. She should have known. When he'd told her that any children they had wouldn't be for him, it had been a warning sign. If he had no room in his heart for children, why would he have room for her?

'So everything you said about me deserving better?' she said huskily. 'That was a lie?'

An expression she couldn't interpret flickered over his face.

'You do deserve better. You deserve better than me, Leonie.'

'But I don't want better.' Her voice was cracking and she couldn't stop it. 'And what makes you think you're not better anyway?'

'What do you think?' His face was set and hard. 'I hurt the people I care about. I destroyed my parents, I nearly destroyed Anna, and I almost destroyed my son.' There was nothing but determination in his gaze. 'I won't destroy you.'

Her heart shredded itself inside her chest, raw pain filling her along with a fury that burned hot. She took a couple of steps towards him, one hand crushing the stems of her bouquet, the other curled in a fist.

'Oh, don't make this about protecting me,' she said, her voice vibrating with anger. 'Or your son. Or Anna. Or even your parents.' She took another step, holding his gaze. 'This is about you, Cristiano. You're not protecting us. You're protecting yourself.'

Something flickered in the depths of his eyes. A sudden spark of his own answering anger. 'And shouldn't I protect myself?' he demanded suddenly, tension in every line of him. 'Shouldn't I decide that love is no longer something I want anything to do with? Losing my son just about destroyed me. I won't put myself through that hell ever again.'

Her throat closed up, her heart aching. She had no answer to that, no logical or reasonable argument to make. Because she could understand it. He had been hurt, and hurt deeply, and that kind of wound didn't heal. Certainly she couldn't heal it.

You will never be enough for him.

Her anger had vanished now, as quickly as it had come, leaving her with nothing but a heavy ache in her chest and tears in her eyes. But still she tried, reaching out to him, trying to reach him in some way.

He caught her by the wrist, holding it gently. 'No, *gatita.*'

His touch and that name. It hurt. It hurt so much.

Her heart filled slowly with agony as tears slid down her cheeks, but she refused to wipe them away. Instead she tugged her hand from his grip and stepped away.

She wouldn't beg. She had her pride. He might not want her, but that didn't change what she felt for him, and she wouldn't pretend, either.

Leonie drew herself up, because to the core of her aching heart she was a fighter and she never gave up. 'I love you, Cristiano Velazquez, Duke of San Lorenzo. I know I can't change the past for you. I can't ever replace what you lost. And I can't heal those wounds in your soul. And I know you don't love me back. But...' She lifted her chin, looked him in the eye. 'None of that matters. You made me see that I was worth something. You made me want something more and you made me think that I deserved to have it. I think we both do.'

A raw expression crossed his face and she couldn't help it. She reached up and touched one cheek lightly, and this time he didn't stop her.

'I just wish... I just wish you believed that, too.'

But it was clear that he didn't.

She dropped her hand and stepped away.

Her poor heart had burned to ash in her chest and there were tears on her cheeks, but her spine was straight as she turned away.

And when she walked out she didn't falter.

CHAPTER ELEVEN

CRISTIANO DIDN'T ARRIVE back at the castle till late that night. Stopping a wedding certainly took less time than planning one, but still it had taken hours of explaining and arranging things until everyone's curiosity had been satisfied.

It would be a scandal, but he didn't care.

He'd told everyone that his bride had taken ill unexpectedly and that the wedding would have to be postponed.

He would naturally cancel everything once the fuss had died down.

The first thing he'd done on arriving back was to see where Leonie was. He'd given orders that she was to be granted anything she wanted, and he'd expected that she'd probably have holed herself up in one of the *castillo*'s other guest rooms.

But what he hadn't expected was to find that she had gone and no one knew where she was. She'd come back from the chapel, disappeared into the bedroom to change and then had apparently vanished into thin air.

When he found out he stormed upstairs to the bedroom, to see if she'd taken anything with her, and was disturbed to find that she hadn't. Not even the new handbag and purse he'd bought her, with all the new bank cards he'd had set up for her.

In fact, she hadn't taken anything at all.

She'd simply…gone.

He got his staff to check every inch of the castle, and then the grounds, and then, when it was clear she wasn't anywhere on the estate, he called his staff to start searching the entire damn country.

He wanted her found and he wouldn't rest until she was.

Why? She's gone and that's how you wanted it. You threw her heart back in her face. Did you really expect her to stick around?

Something tore in his chest, a jagged pain filling him.

He could still feel the imprint of her skin on his fingertips as he'd taken her wrist in his, still see the pain in her eyes and the tears on her cheeks. See her courage as she'd lifted her chin and told him that it didn't matter if he didn't love her. That she loved him anyway.

Dios, she was brave. It wasn't her fault he didn't deserve that love and never would. That he never wanted anything to do with love and the pain it brought, the destruction it wreaked, not ever again.

It's not her fault you're a coward and ended up hurting her anyway.

The tearing pain deepened, widened, winding around his soul.

He shoved himself out of his uncomfortable chair and paced the length of his study, his fingers curled tight around his phone, ready to answer it the second someone called, telling him they'd found her.

He didn't want to think about what she'd said. He only wanted to think about whether or not she was safe. And she would be, surely? She could look after herself. After all, she had for years before he'd taken her from the streets, so why wouldn't she be safe now?

Yet he couldn't relax. Couldn't sit still. Couldn't escape the pain inside him or the cold feeling sitting in his gut.

It's too late. Too late not to love her.

He stopped in the middle of his study, staring out at the darkness beyond the window as the cold reached into his heart.

Because he knew this feeling. It was familiar. He'd felt it once for Anna and for his son. Fear and pain, and longing. An all-consuming rage. An endless well of need that no one could ever fill.

She can. She did.

Cristiano froze, unable to breathe.

Leonie, her face alight with passion as she took his face between her small hands…

Leonie, touching him gently, as if he was precious to her…

Leonie, filling his *castillo* with sunshine and warmth, with her smile and her laughter.

Leonie, whose love wasn't destructive or bitter, despite the long years she'd spent on the streets. Whose love was open and generous and honest, with nothing held back or hidden.

Leonie, who loved him.

She's what you need. What you've always needed.

Everything hurt. It was as if every nerve he had had been unsheathed, sensitive even to the movement of air on his skin.

Love was destructive, but hers wasn't. Why was that?

You know.

Cristiano closed his eyes, facing a truth he'd never wanted to see.

It wasn't love that was destructive, because there had been nothing destructive about the way Leonie had looked at him. Nothing cruel in the way she'd touched him gently as he'd thrown her love back in her face. Nothing angry.

Because it was anger that destroyed. Anger that frightened. Anger that made him bitter and twisted and empty inside.

Anger that made him a coward.

Anger that had hurt her.

He took a shuddering breath.

His proud, beautiful *gatita*. He'd hurt her and she'd simply touched his cheek. Told him that she wished he could see what she saw when she looked at him.

His brave Leonie. Walking away from him with a straight back, unbowed. A fighter in every sense of the word. But alone. Always alone.

Not again.

It was the only thought that made sense. He'd made mistakes in his life—so many mistakes—but the one mistake he'd made, that he kept making over and over again, had been to let his anger win. And he couldn't let it.

Once…just this once…he would let love win.

And he loved her.

Perhaps he had loved her the moment he'd picked her up from the street, seen her staring at him with wide blue eyes, her hair a tangled skein down her back.

He'd tried to deny the emotion, tried to ignore it. Tried to squash it down and contain it because his love had always been such a destructive thing. But he couldn't stop it from pouring through him now, intense and deep. A vast, powerful force.

He remembered this feeling—this helpless, vulnerable feeling. And how he'd fought it, tried to manage it, to grab control where he could. The anguish of wanting something from his parents that they were never going to give, and their instinctive withdrawal from him and his neediness. The pain of it as he'd tried to hold on to Anna. As his son had slipped through his fingers.

The vulnerability that he'd turned into anger, because that was easier and he'd thought it more powerful.

But it wasn't. This feeling was the most powerful. It was everything and he let it pulse through him, overwhelm him, making everything suddenly very, *very* clear.

He had to find her. She thought that they both deserved more. He wasn't sure that was true for him. But she definitely did. And though he had nothing to give her but his own broken, imperfect heart, it was all he had.

He just had to trust it was enough.

Cristiano turned and strode out of the study, his heart on fire, his phone still clutched in his hand.

Leonie waited outside in the garden of the tiny hotel in San Lorenzo, hiding in the darkness. She'd gotten good at it in Paris, and it seemed she still had the gift since no one had spotted her.

It was a long wait. But she had nowhere to go, and nowhere to be, so she stood there until at last the door to the wide terrace opened and a man came out to stand there, gazing out over the garden.

De Riero.

She really didn't know why she was here, or what she intended to do by coming—maybe just see him. Her memories of him were very dim, and they were still dim now. She didn't recognise his face. He was a stranger.

After she'd left the castle, walking to the village in the dark, she'd thought she'd probably have to hitch-hike or stow away in a truck or something in order to leave San Lorenzo. The thought hadn't worried her. She just wanted to get as far away from Cristiano and his cold green eyes as she could.

But then, outside the small village hotel, she'd spotted a tall boy with vaguely familiar features and vivid green eyes and she'd known who it was. And who the tall man beside him must be, too.

And she hadn't been able to go any further.

She hadn't wanted to go into the hotel, so she'd slunk into the gardens and skulked in the shadows, watching the hotel terrace.

Waiting for what, she didn't know, but she hadn't been able to leave all the same.

De Riero reached into his jacket and took out a cigarette, lit it, leaning on the stone parapet of the terrace.

She could step out of the shadows now, reveal herself. Show him that she was still alive—though at the moment 'alive' was relative. Especially when she felt so hollow and empty inside.

What do you want from him?

She didn't know that, either. An apology? An acknowledgement? To be welcomed into his family with open arms?

Her father leaned his elbows on the parapet, his cigarette glowing.

Would he be disappointed if he found out she

wasn't dead after all? Would he be angry with her for disrupting his family? Or would he be grateful? Happy?

Does it matter?

Her throat closed and her chest ached. And she knew the truth. It wouldn't change a thing. Because her heart was broken and it had nothing to do with her father. Nothing to do with his acknowledgement of her or otherwise. She felt nothing for him. Nothing at all.

Because her heart wasn't with him. It was with another man. A man who didn't want it and yet held it in his strong, capable hands anyway.

Whether her father wanted her or not, it wouldn't change that feeling. Wouldn't alter it. Which meant it wasn't this man's acceptance that would make her whole.

Only Cristiano could.

The boy came out onto the terrace, tall and already broad, joining the man. Cristiano's son.

The sounds of their voices carried over the garden, and then their laughter. There was happiness in their voices, an easy affection, and Leonie knew she wasn't going to reveal herself. That she would stay out of it.

That wasn't her family. Not any more.

It felt right to melt away into the shadows and leave them behind.

Her future wasn't with them.

A certain calmness settled inside her, along with determination.

She would find her own family and her own future. She would carve it with her bare hands if she had to, but find it she would. Her future wasn't as a de Riero and it wasn't as a Velazquez, but she would find something else.

She wasn't lost. She'd found herself.

Slowly she walked down the tiny street of San Lorenzo, alone in the dark. And then a car came to a screeching halt beside her and a man leapt out of it.

'Leonie!' a dark, familiar voice said desperately. 'Stop!'

She stilled, staring as Cristiano came towards her, his hair standing up on end, his wedding suit rumpled, the look on his face as raw and naked as she'd ever seen it.

He stopped right in front of her, staring at her, breathing hard. 'Don't leave,' he said hoarsely before she could speak. 'Please don't leave me.'

Shocked tears pricked her eyes, her heart aching and burning. What was he doing here? He'd been very clear on what he'd wanted and it wasn't her, no matter what he was saying now.

Resisting the urge to fling herself into his arms, she drew herself up instead, lifting her chin. 'What are you doing here, Cristiano?' Her voice was hoarse, but she was pleased with how calm she sounded.

'What you said in the chapel…' The look in his eyes burned. 'About deserving more.'

'What?'

'You told me that we both deserved more and that you wished I could believe it, too.' He stared at her. 'I want to know why.'

She blinked her tears back furiously. 'Does it matter?'

He moved then, taking her face between his big, warm palms, his whole body shaking with the force of some deep, powerful emotion. 'Yes,' he said fiercely. 'It matters. It matters more than anything in this entire world.'

His touch was so good. The warmth of it soothed all the broken edges of her soul, making her want to lean into his hands. Give him everything she had.

But he didn't love her, did he? And he never would. And that wasn't enough for her any more. It just wasn't.

'Why?' She forced away the tears. 'Why does it matter to you?'

The street lights glossed his black hair, made his eyes glitter strangely. 'Because you matter, *gatita*. You matter to me.'

Her breath caught—everything caught. 'What?' The question came out in a hoarse whisper.

'I came back and you were gone, and no one knew where you were.'

There was something bright and fierce in his expression.

'I couldn't rest and I couldn't sit still. I was afraid for you. And I knew it was too late. I've been trying not to love you, my little *gatita*. I've been trying not to care, trying to protect myself. But you're so easy to love, and I fell for you without even realising that I'd fallen.'

His thumbs moved gently over her cheekbones, wiping away tears she hadn't known were there.

'I resisted so hard. Love is so destructive, and I've hurt so many people. But it was you who showed me another way. You made me see that it wasn't love that destroyed things, it was anger. My anger.'

He loved her? He really loved her?

Everything took on a strange, slightly unreal quality, and she had to put her hands up and close her fingers around his strong wrists to make sure he was real.

'How?' she asked hoarsely. 'I didn't do—'

'You've spent years on the streets. Years fighting for your survival. Years with nothing and no one. And, yes, you're angry—but you haven't let it define you. You haven't let it make you bitter. No, it's your love that defines you. Your joy and your passion. And that's what I want, *mi corazón*. I want you to teach me how to love like that…teach me how to love *you* like that.'

She was trembling, and she didn't want to look away from him in case this wasn't real. In case he disappeared, as all the good things in her life seemed to do.

'You don't need me to teach you,' she whispered in a scratchy voice. 'You already know how to love, Cristiano. You just have to let go of your anger.'

He said nothing for a long moment, staring down into her face, holding her as if he was afraid of exactly the same thing she was: that this thing they were both within touching distance of would vanish and never come back.

'Is that what you see?' he asked roughly. 'When you look at me? How do I deserve anything if anger is all there is?'

His face blurred as more tears filled her vision and she had to blink them away fiercely. 'That's not all there is. You're a good man, a kind man. A man who feels things deeply and intensely. A protective man desperate for something to protect.'

She slid her hands up his wrists, covering the backs of his where they cupped her face.

'A man who wants someone to be his—and you deserve that, Cristiano. More, I think you need it.'

'I don't know that I did to deserve it. But I'm willing to spend my life trying.' His eyes burned with an intense green fire. 'Will you be mine, Leonie?'

'You don't have to try,' she said thickly. 'And I'm already yours. I've never been anyone else's.'

'Then please come back to me, *gatita*.' He searched her face as if he couldn't quite believe her. 'Please come home.'

But she didn't need him to plead. She'd already decided.

She went up on her toes and pressed her mouth to his, and when his arms came around her and held her tight she became whole.

With him she would never be homeless.

Because he was her home.

EPILOGUE

CRISTIANO PAID THE bill and pushed back his chair, standing up. The restaurant was very crowded and no one was looking at them, too involved with their own conversations to pay attention to the tall man with green eyes and the other, much younger man opposite him, who also stood, and who also had the same green eyes.

The lunch had gone surprisingly well, but it was too soon for an embrace so Cristiano only held out his hand, looking his son in the eye. 'It was good to meet you, Alexander.'

His son frowned, looked down at his extended hand, and then, after a moment, reached out and took it, shaking it firmly. 'I can't call you Papá— you know that, right?'

'Of course not,' Cristiano said easily. 'You already have one of those.'

De Riero—which wasn't what Cristiano had either wanted or chosen, but he couldn't change what had happened twenty years ago. All he could do was let go of his anger and accept it.

It hadn't been easy, but he'd done it. With a little help from Leonie, naturally enough.

In fact, that he'd made contact with his son at all had been all down to her. After a few years—after their lives had settled down and his son had become an adult in his own right—she'd encouraged Cristiano and supported him to reach out.

De Riero hadn't liked it, but something must have mellowed him over the years, because when Alexander had asked him about his parentage he apparently hadn't denied that Cristiano was his father.

He'd even tried to make contact with Leonie, when word had got out about the identity of Cristiano's wife. She hadn't wanted to take that step yet, but Cristiano knew she would one day. When she was ready.

As for Alexander... Cristiano didn't know what de Riero had told the boy about him, but clearly nothing too bad, since he had eventually agreed to meet him.

It had been tense initially, but Alexander had eventually relaxed. As had Cristiano.

'I'd like to meet with you again,' Cristiano said after they'd shaken hands. 'Lunch? Once a month, say?'

The young man nodded, looking serious. 'I think I'd like that.' He paused, giving Cristiano another measuring look. 'You're not what I expected,' he said at last.

Cristiano raised a brow. 'What did you expect?'

'I don't know. You're just...' Alexander lifted a shoulder. 'Easier to talk to than I thought you'd be.'

Something in Cristiano's heart—a wound that hadn't ever fully healed—felt suddenly a little less painful.

He smiled. 'I'll take that.'

Ten minutes later, after Alexander had left, he stepped out of the restaurant and onto the footpath— and was nearly bowled over by two small figures.

'Papá!' the little boy yelled, flinging himself at his father, closely followed by his red-haired sister.

The pain in Cristiano's heart suddenly dissolved as if it had never been. He opened his arms, scooping both children up. They squealed, his daughter gripping onto his hair while his son grabbed his shirt.

It was soon apparent that both of them had been eating ice cream and had got it all over their hands.

'They're too big for that,' Leonie said, coming up behind them, her face alight with amusement. 'And look what Carlos has done to your shirt.'

Cristiano only laughed. 'That's what washing machines are for.'

She rolled her eyes. She'd lost nothing of her fire and spark over the past five years, coming into her own as his duchess. Not only had she proved adept at helping him manage the San Lorenzo estate, as well as becoming the driving force behind various charities aimed at helping children on the streets, she'd also proved herself to be a talented artist. Luckily she used oils and canvas these days, rather than spray cans and cars.

She was looking at him now in that way he loved. Sharp and direct. Seeing through him and into his heart. 'How did it go?' she asked.

He grinned. 'It went well. Very well indeed.'

Her eyes glinted and he realised they were full of tears.

'I'm so glad.'

His beautiful, beautiful *gatita*. She had worried for him.

Cristiano put down the twins and ignored their complaints, gathering his wife in his arms. 'He wants to meet again. Lunch, once a month.'

'Oh, Cristiano.' Leonie put her arms around his neck and buried her face in his shirt.

He put his hands in her hair, stroking gently, his heart full as he soothed his wife while two of his children tugged at his jacket, oblivious, and the third…

The third he'd find out more about soon.

It was enough. It was more than he'd ever thought he'd have.

After winter there was summer.

And after rain there was sunshine.

After anger and grief and loss there was love.

Always and for ever love.

Cristiano kissed his wife. 'Come, Leonie Velazquez. Let's go home.'

* * * * *

Adored The Spaniard's Wedding Revenge?
You're sure to enjoy these other stories by
Jackie Ashenden!

Demanding His Hidden Heir
Claiming His One-Night Child
Crowned at the Desert King's Command

All available now!

WE HOPE YOU ENJOYED
THIS BOOK FROM

⬡ HARLEQUIN

PRESENTS

Escape to exotic locations where passion knows no bounds.

Welcome to the glamorous lives of royals and billionaires, where passion knows no bounds. Be swept into a world of luxury, wealth and exotic locations.

8 NEW BOOKS AVAILABLE EVERY MONTH!

HPHALO2020

COMING NEXT MONTH FROM

⊞ HARLEQUIN
PRESENTS

Available May 19, 2020

#3817 CINDERELLA'S ROYAL SECRET
Once Upon a Temptation
by Lynne Graham

For innocent cleaner Izzy, accidentally interrupting her most exclusive client, Sheikh Rafiq, coming out of the shower is mortifying...yet their instantaneous attraction leads to the most amazing night of her life! But then she does a pregnancy test...

#3818 BEAUTY AND HER ONE-NIGHT BABY
Once Upon a Temptation
by Dani Collins

The first time Scarlett sees Javiero after their impassioned night together, she's in labor with his baby! She won't accept empty vows, even if she can't forget the pleasure they shared...and could share again!

#3819 SHY QUEEN IN THE ROYAL SPOTLIGHT
Once Upon a Temptation
by Natalie Anderson

To retain the throne he's sacrificed everything for, Alek *must* choose a bride. Hester's inner fire catches his attention. Alek sees the queen that she could truly become—but the real question is, can *she*?

#3820 CLAIMED IN THE ITALIAN'S CASTLE
Once Upon a Temptation
by Caitlin Crews

When innocent piano-playing Angelina must marry enigmatic Benedetto Franceschi, she *should* be terrified—his reputation precedes him. But their electrifying chemistry forges an unspoken connection. Dare she hope he could become the husband she deserves?

HPCNMRA0520

#3821 EXPECTING HIS BILLION-DOLLAR SCANDAL
Once Upon a Temptation
by Cathy Williams

Luca relished the fact his fling with Cordelia was driven by desire, not his wealth. Now their baby compels him to bring her into his sumptuous world. But to give Cordelia his heart? It's a price he can't pay...

#3822 TAMING THE BIG BAD BILLIONAIRE
Once Upon a Temptation
by Pippa Roscoe

Ella may be naive, but she's no pushover. Discovering Roman's lies, she can't pretend their passion-filled marriage never happened. He might see himself as a big bad wolf, but she knows he could be so much more...

#3823 THE FLAW IN HIS MARRIAGE PLAN
Once Upon a Temptation
by Tara Pammi

Family is *everything* to tycoon Vincenzo. The man who ruined his mother's life will pay. Vincenzo will wed his enemy's adopted daughter: Alessandra. The flaw in his plan? Their fiery attraction... and his need to protect her.

#3824 HIS INNOCENT'S PASSIONATE AWAKENING
Once Upon a Temptation
by Melanie Milburne

If there's a chance that marrying Artie will give his grandfather the will to live, Luca *must* do it. But he's determined to resist temptation. Until their scorching wedding kiss stirs the beauty to sensual new life!

YOU CAN FIND MORE INFORMATION ON UPCOMING HARLEQUIN TITLES, FREE EXCERPTS AND MORE AT HARLEQUIN.COM.

HPCNMRB0520

SPECIAL EXCERPT FROM

⟨H⟩HARLEQUIN
PRESENTS

*The first time Scarlett sees Javiero after their
impassioned night together she's in labour with his
baby! But she won't accept empty vows—even if she
can't forget the pleasure they shared...and could
share again!*

*Read on for a sneak preview of Dani Collins's
next story for Harlequin Presents,*
Beauty and Her One-Night Baby.

Scarlett dropped her phone with a clatter.

She had been trying to call Kiara. Now she was taking in the
livid claw marks across Javiero's face, each pocked on either side
with the pinpricks of recently removed stitches. His dark brown
hair was longer than she'd ever seen it, perhaps gelled back from
the widow's peak at some point this morning, but it was mussed
and held a jagged part. He wore a black eye patch like a pirate, its
narrow band cutting a thin stripe across his temple and into his hair.

Maybe that's why his features looked as though they had been
set askew? His mouth was...not right. His upper lip was uneven
and the claw marks drew lines through his unkempt stubble all the
way down into his neck.

That was dangerously close to his jugular! Dear God, he had
nearly been killed.

She grasped at the edge of the sink, trying to stay on her feet
while she grew so light-headed at the thought of him dying that she
feared she would faint.

The ravages of his attack weren't what made him look so
forbidding and grim, though, she computed through her haze of

panic and anguish. No. The contemptuous glare in his one eye was for her. For this.

He flicked another outraged glance at her middle.

"I thought we were meeting in the boardroom." His voice sounded gravelly. Damaged as well? Or was that simply his true feelings toward her now? Deadly and completely devoid of any of the sensual admiration she'd sometimes heard in his tone.

Not that he'd ever been particularly warm toward her. He'd been aloof, indifferent, irritated, impatient, explosively passionate. Generous in the giving of pleasure. Of compliments. Then cold as she left. Disapproving. Malevolent.

Damningly silent.

And now he was…what? Ignoring that she was as big as a barn?

Her arteries were on fire with straight adrenaline, her heart pounding and her brain spinning with the way she was having to switch gears so fast. Her eyes were hot and her throat tight. Everything in her wanted to scream *help me*, but she'd been in enough tight spots to know this was all on her. Everything was always on her. She fought to keep her head and get through the next few minutes before she moved on to the next challenge.

Which was just a tiny trial called childbirth, but she would worry about that when she got to the hospital.

As the tingle of a fresh contraction began to pang in her lower back, she tightened her grip on the edge of the sink and gritted her teeth, trying to ignore the coming pain and hang on to what dregs of dignity she had left.

"I'm in labor," she said tightly. "It's yours."

Don't miss
Beauty and Her One-Night Baby.

*Available June 2020 wherever
Harlequin Presents books and ebooks are sold.*

Harlequin.com

Copyright © 2020 by Dani Collins

HPEXP0520

Get 4 FREE REWARDS!

We'll send you 2 FREE Books
<u>plus</u> 2 FREE Mystery Gifts.

PRESENTS

**Indian Prince's
Hidden Son**

USA TODAY BESTSELLING AUTHOR
LYNNE GRAHAM

PRESENTS

**The Greek's
One-Night Heir**

USA TODAY BESTSELLING AUTHOR
NATALIE ANDERSON

Harlequin Presents books
feature the glamorous
lives of royals and
billionaires in a world of
exotic locations, where
passion knows no bounds.

FREE
Value Over
$20

YES! Please send me 2 FREE Harlequin Presents novels and my 2 FREE gifts (gifts are worth about $10 retail). After receiving them, if I don't wish to receive any more books, I can return the shipping statement marked "cancel." If I don't cancel, I will receive 6 brand-new novels every month and be billed just $4.55 each for the regular-print edition or $5.80 each for the larger-print edition in the U.S., or $5.49 each for the regular-print edition or $5.99 each for the larger-print edition in Canada. That's a savings of at least 11% off the cover price! It's quite a bargain! Shipping and handling is just 50¢ per book in the U.S. and $1.25 per book in Canada.* I understand that accepting the 2 free books and gifts places me under no obligation to buy anything. I can always return a shipment and cancel at any time. The free books and gifts are mine to keep no matter what I decide.

Choose one: ☐ **Harlequin Presents**   ☐ **Harlequin Presents**
                    Regular-Print   **Larger-Print**
                    (106/306 HDN GNWY)   (176/376 HDN GNWY)

Name (please print)

Address   Apt. #

City   State/Province   Zip/Postal Code

Mail to the **Reader Service:**
IN U.S.A.: P.O. Box 1341, Buffalo, NY 14240-8531
IN CANADA: P.O. Box 603, Fort Erie, Ontario L2A 5X3

Want to try 2 free books from another series! Call 1-800-873-8635 or visit www.ReaderService.com.

*Terms and prices subject to change without notice. Prices do not include sales taxes, which will be charged (if applicable) based on your state or country of residence. Canadian residents will be charged applicable taxes. Offer not valid in Quebec. This offer is limited to one order per household. Books received may not be as shown. Not valid for current subscribers to Harlequin Presents books. All orders subject to approval. Credit or debit balances in a customer's account(s) may be offset by any other outstanding balance owed by or to the customer. Please allow 4 to 6 weeks for delivery. Offer available while quantities last.

Your Privacy—The Reader Service is committed to protecting your privacy. Our Privacy Policy is available online at www.ReaderService.com or upon request from the Reader Service. We make a portion of our mailing list available to reputable third parties that offer products we believe may interest you. If you prefer that we not exchange your name with third parties, or if you wish to clarify or modify your communication preferences, please visit us at www.ReaderService.com/consumerschoice or write to us at Reader Service Preference Service, P.O. Box 9062, Buffalo, NY 14240-9062. Include your complete name and address.

HP20R